The BiG SWaMP

Raymond D.
Schofield

A Wildlife
Biologist's
Lifetime of
Adventures

DESTINY
Pentwater, Michigan

Part One of this novel is based on actual events. Part Two is a product of the imagination of the author. Although many of the characters are real people, liberties have been taken in many instances as to their actual behavior. The story has no purpose other than to entertain the reader.

Published by Destiny
5882 Long Bridge Road
Pentwater, Michigan 49449

Publisher's Cataloging-in-Publication Data
Schofield, Raymond D.
    The big swamp: a wildlife biologist's lifetime of adventures / Raymond D. Schofield. – Pentwater, Mich.: Destiny, 2000.
        p. cm.
    ISBN 0-9676025-0-5
        1. Naturalists—fiction. I. Title.
PS3569.C546 B54   2000   99-66655
813' .54   dc—21   CIP

PROJECT COORDINATION BY JENKINS GROUP, INC.

03 02 01 00 ◆ 5 4 3 2 1

Printed in the United States of America

To Jeanne, "My Little French Girl"

Jeanne entered my life at a time I was deeply troubled. In her straightforward way she soon had me thinking about important things, rather than simply dwelling on my personal problems. She gave me 25 years of peace, contentment, and most of all love. We both retired on the same day (her idea). Thank God for those first 11 years of retirement. We were able to accomplish so much together, including getting the first draft of this book down on paper. During the last two years of her life, we both learned what real love is all about. It takes two to fight cancer. No one should have to do it alone.

I miss her greatly, but she taught me how to cope with life's problems and I will be okay.

Foreword

IT WAS PLEASING AND AN HONOR WHEN IT WAS SUGGESTED THAT I write a foreword to this book. Frankly, I didn't think that Ray would ever finish it so I wouldn't have to fulfill my promise.

But, lo and behold, he did! Hence, my few words as an introduction. I must say I really like Ray's tale of a fictional hare hunt, because it reminded me of hounds we owned and hunts we shared many years ago.

Ray is in his seventies, as am I. In fact, he is two years younger than me. He and I hunted together for many years until too many miles separated us. I am still his friend.

This book reflects a hunting philosophy that is infrequently in evidence today. Part of his story is fact, part is fiction, but is difficult to tell where one starts and the other ends because they are woven into a story of friends that grew up in an era when hunting was more than just a sport because it put needed food on the table.

Finally, Ray's basic and thoughtful philosophy toward life and the out-of-doors is reflected in his prayer to our God in the final pages of this book.

I hope the reader will enjoy this book as much as I have.

PETE PETOSKEY

Part I

CHAPTER ONE

ACOOL LIGHT RAIN WAS FALLING AS THE BUCK FAWN FOL-
lowed his mother, a large doe, out to the edge of a
marsh. The deer wanted to get a drink before bedding
down for the day. Bringing up the rear was his sibling, a lively
doe fawn. Both were now almost one year old.

Spring peepers filled the morning air with their music. High
overhead a Wilson's snipe's winnowing added to the morning's
magic. At the far end of the marsh a hen mallard announced to
her mate that she was off her nest and would appreciate a little
attention.

The fawns were used to the sounds of the marsh, as they had
spent their entire life within a mile or two from the spot where
they now drank. When they raised their heads, they found
themselves all alone as the old doe had already headed back
toward high ground. The doe's action came as no surprise to the
young deer because they were aware of a gradual loosening of
the close parental bonds. This time was no different than several others in recent weeks. Again, they relied on their sharp sense

of smell to pick up the trail of their mother. It was several minutes before they found her, already bedded down for the day.

Dense lowland brush, alder, and dogwood covered the bedding site. Dead marsh grass made the immediate area a perfect hiding place for the three deer. The fawns laid down beside the doe and prepared to spend the day. They knew it would be almost dark before they would venture out of the thicket. Perhaps they would be permitted to get up and stretch their legs once in a while, but they had already learned that their security depended on staying close to the old doe. Yet her actions lately seemed to say," It's time for you year-old fawns to head out on your own." She knew that in a couple more weeks she would give birth to more fawns, probably twins again.

The six-year-old doe had been a good teacher. The fawns were well prepared to strike out into the world. And in a few days the old doe simply vanished, and the yearlings were left to fend for themselves. If everything worked out as normal, the doe fawn would be allowed to rejoin her mother's family group sometime in early fall. The young buck would have nothing to do with that, as he had his own ideas about his future. Before the summer was out he would be guided by strong hormonal urges that altered his physical and mental state. Even now, he had an uncontrollable urge to leave familiar surroundings and head off into strange country. A few days later he did just that.

Little did he know that he was destined to play a key role in a human drama, filled with deep-seated emotions, that only human beings could experience. After traveling in a northerly direction for several days, he came to much different country than that where he had spent his first year of life. He had been reared in an agricultural area. In fact, he had been born in a hay field and at an early age had learned about farm dogs and other hazards associated with living in close proximity to humans. Now he had to call on all his resources in order to survive this most dangerous journey. Hide in dense cover during most of the daylight hours and venture out only as darkness was fast closing in. He fed as he traveled, constantly alert to possible dangers. A mistake now could be fatal. Fortunately, he was "road wise" as several busy highways had to be crossed.

He recalled other lessons passed on by his mother. Select your bedding area well in advance of the first light of dawn. Face any air movements and always leave an escape route. If danger forces leaving the bedding area, don't head off for the next county. Just move far enough to escape the immediate danger and then bed down again. He had learned many of these things by following his mother during his first firearm deer season. The old doe had moved her little family out in the middle of a large cornfield. They usually spent the day bedded down in a small pothole, too small for hunters to even consider checking out. Fortunately, it was a wet fall and the corn remained standing until the end of the deer season. On a couple days snow covered the ground, so the old doe laid tight. The fawns learned their lessons well.

Now as the young buck moved north, he left the familiar farm country. Abandoned farm fields and rolling ridges now dominated the landscape. It was obvious that the healthy stands of oak, black cherry, and hickory found throughout much of southern Lower Michigan's forested areas were absent. The soils here were poor and the fields were growing up to briers, sumac, and aspen. Even the oaks on the drier ridges were stunted with clumps of aspen, witch hazel, and thornapple dominating the site. If the land could talk it could tell stories of broken dreams, broken promises, and worse.

It had been a warm day, so the young deer left his daytime bed a little early. As the last rays of daylight faded, he reached the top of a large hill and looked north toward the lowland ahead. It was a sight he had never seen before. Stretching before him was vast forested lowland, his first view of a northern conifer swamp. A great sense of security crept over him as he crossed a gravel road and entered the swamp just west of a small stream that flowed toward the south. The water made a soft tinkling sound as it flowed over cedar roots and windfalls as it made its constant march toward the Chippewa River, fifteen miles to the south.

The deer moved over to the creek and took his first drink from the crystal clear water. At that moment something told him that he had reached the end of his journey. The big swamp offered deep security and the surrounding land provided a wide variety of habitat types. Even some small farms were mixed in. The location was excellent deer habitat, and the young buck was aware that he was not alone.

CHAPTER TWO

EARLY SETTLERS, WHO MOVED INTO THIS PART OF MID-Michigan to homestead the land, just went a few miles too far north. Of course, the promise of land easily cleared following logging of the pine forests and subsequent forest fires, helped to convince them that this was the place to carve their future out of the wilderness. The tremendous stands of pine with northern hardwoods (on the more fertile uplands) and large white cedar in the lowland swamps made the entire area attractive to lumbermen. Some made huge fortunes by logging off these old growth forests. The pine logs were floated down the Muskegon River, the hardwood carted off to thriving furniture factories, and the giant cedar trees were cut to fuel local shingle mills.

Most everyone believed that this period of prosperity would go on forever. Unfortunately, this was not true. Prime timberlands were soon laid to waste. Some think that forest fires played a more important role than what has been recorded. But at any rate, Mid-Michigan's vast forest resources were soon gone. And the farmers who followed had little trouble pulling the pine stumps out of the sandy soil and establishing small homesteads. More than riches, they sought independence and a safe place to establish roots and raise their families.

My grandparents were part of this movement into central Michigan. Fortunately, they settled down on the more fertile soils in Isabella County. My mother's parents located near Winn and my father's west of Rosebush. The soil was good and with a lot of work both farms turned out good crops and livestock. My father had farming in his blood, but he also developed into an excellent carpenter. He was sought out to build barns, silos, and other farm buildings. Soon after marrying my mother in 1903 they moved to California and he tried his hand at building oil derricks. They were made out of wood in those days.

Children came so fast that my parents were overwhelmed. Life on a small Michigan farm looked better and better, so in 1911 they came home. They first settled on a small farm southeast of a big swamp, now called Deadman Swamp. Later, after moving to two or three other places, they purchased a 120-acre farm on the Maple Grove Road on the north side of the swamp. In 1927, their tenth and last child, a girl, was born. I was born two years earlier in 1925. Six girls and four boys completed the family.

We were one big, happy family. As far as I know, my parents never accepted the Dole, as welfare was known as in those days. I never saw my parents have a serious argument. Perhaps they did, but if so they always kept their differences to themselves. Big families were assets in those days. The boys helped with the farming and the girls helped Ma with a huge garden and canning. With all the strong backs around Pa had time to pursue his building trade and it provided a more stable income than the meager crops coming off the sandy, stony, soils.

We kids learned to live off the land, especially number nine, as I became the hunter in the family after my two older brothers left home. Our garden, livestock, a few apple trees, and the products nature provided from the fields and woods were staples in our everyday diets. Ma was proud of the shelves in the basement lined with quart cans of blackberries, strawberries, cherries, beets, string beans, tomatoes, applesauce, beef, and from my contribution, venison and rabbits. We always entered the winter with our basement well stocked. Apples were carefully wrapped in tissue paper and placed on a cool, dry shelf. Over in one corner, on the dirt floor, were several bushels of potatoes and carrots. Two ten-gallon crocks finished up our storehouse. One was filled with dill pickles and one contained sauerkraut. We kids liked to lift the plate that held the kraut down and sample how it was doing. And our family did all this without electricity or a farm tractor. We farmed with horses.

My mother lived to be ninety-eight years old. She was very proud that all ten kids graduated from Farwell High School. Five even graduated from college. Ma got her teacher certificate from the Normal School in Mt. Pleasant, now Central Michigan University, in 1901. She was only sixteen at the time. Even though my father had little formal education, I recall that he was very good in mathematics. He needed arithmetic to calculate the complex angles used in the building trade and he was very fast with the calculations.

My dad died in 1938 at fifty-three years of age. I was only thirteen at the time.

CHAPTER THREE

HOW DID IT ALL COME TO PASS THAT I BECAME A DYED-IN-the-wool hunter? Perhaps more than anything it was because of a dog. One Saturday, in early spring, Pa returned home from a job in southeast Michigan at Lake Orion, where he was "building second homes for the rich folks from the Detroit area." In the back seat of our old Chevy was a cardboard box with two beagle puppies curled up on one of his old shirts. "Hey! Son come and look what I brought home."

Being only five, I was naturally very excited. "Can I take them out of the box, Pa?" I asked.

"Sure," my dad replied, "but just be careful how you handle them, as they are pretty young yet." Thus began my love affair with beagles. I was so excited I hardly heard my dad add, "The rabbits around here better watch out when these dogs get a little bigger."

The next day Pa explained to the family that the little puppies weren't ours to keep. They belonged to a Mr. Richey, a professional dog trainer, who raised and trained beagles to run in field trials. "Don't get too attached to them now, as he will want them back after we get them running rabbits." Pa's warning was in vain. I had already decided that those little pups were about the nicest thing in the world. Even Old Faithful Sport, our farm collie, had to play second fiddle. Apparently, Mr. Richey was having trouble finding enough time to train all the dogs in his kennel, so he had asked Pa to take a couple back to the farm where they could run rabbits almost every day. Perhaps we could even earn a little money caring for the dogs and Pa knew that we kids would take good care of them.

The female was named Queenie and the male was Bob. Both were well-bred hounds from field champion stock. Mr. Richey had litter registered them at birth and they were already eight weeks old. My dad promised that they would be running at six months, and they were. Deer were scarce around the area in those days, so it was easy to keep the beagles from running "trash game," as Mr. Richey called deer. Pa built a large outdoor pen with chicken wire and a warm, comfortable doghouse. The doghouse had a flat roof so the little beagles could sit on top and watch the comings and goings on the farm.

As they grew, they soon learned to watch the house in the hopes that Pa would come out and let them run a little. We did-n't dare to let them out. Only my dad did that, with a real ritu-al. "Want to go huntin'? Want to go huntin'?" he would holler at the little dogs. It wasn't long before he was taking them on short walks to the back "forty" where a cottontail rabbit could often be jumped and the dogs soon learned what it was all about.

By late August, Pa started to let Queenie and Bob run out to the back of the farm and search out their own rabbits. Then the brushy woods margin would ring out with hound music. Pa would sit on the back porch, smoking his pipe, with a satisfied look on his face and just listen to the little beagles, doing what they were bred to do. Quite often I would join him and he would explain how the chase was going. Pa never hunted much, but he certainly had a deep love for hounds, both beagles and foxhounds.

Sometimes a driven rabbit would leave the brushy woods and cross a small field to reach a swale southeast of the house. Around the willow swale they would go. First, the rabbit and then close behind the yowling dogs, announcing to the world, "I got him! I got him!" If the rabbit was pushed too hard, or just got tired of running, it would hole up in a stone pile on the southwest edge of the swale. Old woodchuck holes were also harbors of refuge for the poor rabbits that didn't appreciate the pesky beagles. When a rabbit went underground or in the stone pile the little dogs would mill around for a minute before heading out to find a more cooperative rabbit.

Thus went the training, day after day. "Hounds don't learn anything cooped up or on the end of a chain," Pa often said. Obviously, he was proud of the way the dogs were progressing and those beagles soon became the talk of the neighborhood. Meanwhile, the operations of the farm went on. Crops were planted and later cultivated. Hay had to be cut and mowed away in the barn. The cows had to be milked twice a day. I noticed that Pa did less and less of the heavy work. He sat around, smoked his pipe and seemed to be deep in thought. Never did I hear him complain about how he felt.

Sure, I was glad that he didn't return to his carpenter job at Lake Orion. But with the excitement of the new dogs and additional chores loaded on me and the rest of the family, I didn't think about Pa's situation. My older brothers simply took over all the heavy work and the routine of operating the farm went on. Perhaps the older children knew, but I didn't. Pa had suffered a serious heart attack and the doctor had ordered him to take it easy for a few months to see how things worked out. Ma and two of the older sisters kept busy with cooking, canning, and tending a large garden. Sometimes, I hated that big cook stove in the kitchen. It was always too hot in the summer and I never knew any stove that could burn wood like that big monster! You see, it was my job to keep the wood box full, and wood for the range had to be split just so. You couldn't jam any big chunks under the round lids on the heating surface.

During the heat of the summer, Pa only let the dogs run during the cool evening hours. "Makes it easier on the dogs and the rabbits," he said. I already knew that all farm families had plans for the surplus game animals living in the vicinity. They were destined to be shot and eaten. And the new beagles would be expected to help with the harvest.

Other good rabbit dogs lived in the neighborhood. Old Buck made his home with the Smedley family just one mile to the east. Buck was much larger than our little beagles, perhaps some foxhound among his ancestors. He really drove a rabbit, so Pa kept the little thirteen-inch dogs from running with Buck. He didn't want them to develop bad habits by running behind on a chase.

Spot was another beagle that belonged to the Rogers, who lived only a half mile east. Spot had a loud bugle voice, but he didn't get to run enough as the older Rogers boys were away on factory jobs in the city. But on the weekends during the hunting season, they made it home. Then you could hear Spot's loud hound music ringing back by the railroad tracks behind the Rogers house. Often the boys would cross the tracks and hunt the big swamp. I already knew that chances were that a different kind of rabbit was then up and running. Locals called them "jack-rabbits", but they were snowshoe or varying hares. "Varying" because they turned completely white in the wintertime.

Pa kept our dogs out of the big swamp and even discouraged them from running in the lowland conifers on the north side of the tracks behind our farm. "Those jacks will take them clear out of hearing and they aren't ready for that yet. Besides, they might get on a deer back there by Deadman Lake. You can hunt those white rabbits when you get a little older," Pa said.

A mile and a half south of us, on the west side of the big swamp, lived another family with a bunch of young boys, who seemed to be hunting all the time. They really knew how to live off the land. This was a necessity, as they had no tillable land. Of course they had a few milk cows, a few beef critters, pigs, and chickens. But, most importantly, they always had two or three good beagles.

"None of the Shaar family will ever starve to death," Pa observed one night as the family was discussing the coming hunting season. "Those boys are good hunters, good shots, and with that bunch of rabbit dogs there will always be plenty of meat around."

Later, as a teenager, I found out what my dad meant. Anytime I hunted more than a mile south of the farm I almost always ran into Jack, Pete or Ted Shaar (or all three of them) out in the woods harvesting the game. And they were good at it!

They not only shot the cottontails and jacks, but they shot the partridge, too. We called the ruffed grouse, partridge or just pats. I knew you had to be able to handle a shotgun to consistently bag pats, and I didn't even try until I was thirteen and armed with a bigger gun than my little .410. The Shaars always had time to stop to talk to me and offer some good hunting tips. They never crowded in on me when my little hound was running. I'm sure they knew I needed all the breaks in the world to put that cottontail in my game bag. I found them to be delightful people, and even though they never knew, I'm sure they left me with some lasting impressions of what sportsmanship was all about.

CHAPTER FOUR

As the weather grew colder, Pa let the beagles run for hours at a time. As Queenie and Bob had run with no other dogs, they had great faith in each other's ability to follow the rabbit line. At a check (that is a term used by beaglers to indicate that a rabbit had changed directions and the dogs temporarily lost the trail) when one announced, " I got it," the other promptly harked in.

It was a real pleasure watching and listening to those hounds run. Both dogs had "chop" voices. Queenie's was bell-like with Bob's being a little deeper-throated. Of course, I was too young to fully appreciate how good they were. Only Mr. Ritchey would be able to judge that.

And sure enough, in early October, the inevitable happened. A new Oldsmobile pulled into our farmyard and a big man, dressed in the finest hunting clothes, got out. It was Mr. Richey. Perhaps Pa knew he was coming, but we kids certainly didn't. I've often wondered why he hadn't tried to break the news to me before hand, but he didn't. Pa greeted the stranger like a long lost friend, while I just wanted to see him get back in the car and drive away.

"Well, Elmer, how's that brace of hounds doing?" Mr. Richey finally asked.

"Just great, George," Pa replied.

Then the two men took out their pipes, sat on the back porch and began to discuss things that small ears weren't supposed to hear. I knew my place, so promptly found something else to do. Over the years I've learned what took place, so I will try to continue the conversation.

"Elmer, I want to do a little hunting this fall as I'm a firm believer that all hounds should have a few rabbits shot ahead of them. Not all dog handlers agree with me, but my beagles always place pretty well in the big trials," Mr. Ritchey explained.

"Well, I don't know anything about field trials, but I've seen a lot of rabbit dogs in my life and these two are the best of the bunch," Pa added.

Pa knew it was time to discuss the cost of keeping the dogs for the past seven months, but remained silent. He always believed in letting the other man make his move. He wanted to have the little hounds do well in the big time, but he had mixed emotions about letting them go. Mr. Ritchey's offer wasn't long in coming.

"Elmer, this hasn't been my best year and I'm a little short of cash. I'll pay you what you think would be a fair amount for the dog food and any other expenses, but I'd like to see you keep the female hound for your troubles."

Pa had trouble hiding his enthusiasm for the offer. He knew the older boys would be returning home in a week or so to do some hunting and he knew how disappointed they would be to find both dogs gone. Before now they had always hunted with neighborhood friends with dogs but that's not the same as hunting with your own. Besides my dad knew that Queenie was destined to be a really great hound, because she already was.

"Don't make a mistake, George, better try them out before you decide which dog to take," Pa said.

Mr. Richey then knew that a fair deal had been made.

"Well, let's put it this way, Elmer, we beaglers put a lot of effort into finishing a hound. Even with the best breeding only one in a hundred or more dogs will make it to the field champion level, no matter how hard we try. With a field champion male we can put him up for stud and make a little money. Sure, it's nice to own a field champion female, but my reason for selecting the male is related to the economics of the situation."

He went on to explain how tough the competition gets with "triple field champion dogs", all ancestors on both sides sired by field champions. It was easy to see that Mr. Richey loved the field trial business, and with that discussion out of the way he returned to the car with the lead that had two collars dangling from the end. In a minute he returned with two brand new collars, each with its separate leather leash attached.

"This guy didn't have any money?" Pa thought. It's just that he wanted his old friend to own a real beagle.

He handed Pa a leash and collar and said, "Teach your boys to always keep that little hound on a leash when walking down the road. These crazy cars get too many of our best dogs." With that he put the other lead on Bob and led him over to the Oldsmobile and gently placed him in a fancy dog box on the back seat. That's the last time we saw that little hound that we all thought had been slated to become a field champion.

Only a month later he was dead, a victim of an automobile, in spite of the always-careful Mr. Richey. We all felt bad when we learned of Bob's death, and Pa was quick to offer his friend Queenie in replacement. Mr. Richey would not even consider that possibility, so we all breathed easier when we were sure that our little beagle was ours to keep.

In those days, October 15 marked the start of the small game hunting season. After Queenie lost her brace mate, Pa had let Sport, the family collie, run rabbits with her. Another dog always provides the competition that a young hound needs. Everyone knew that Sport would head straight for the house if anyone tried to sneak out with a gun. He even hid under the bed during thunderstorms. But for now, he really had fun yapping along with Queenie's rich tenor chop.

After the hunting season opened, my older brothers, who were now married and living away from the farm, would come out and take Queenie home for two days of hard hunting on the weekends. She spent every Saturday and Sunday with Bernard, who usually hunted with Elmer (Jr.), and Don (a brother-in-law). Queenie did what she was bred to do, drive rabbits to the gun.

Her fame spread far and wide, along with the inevitable question, "Hey, Elmer, how about letting me borrow your dog during the week, when the boys aren't using her?"

Going back to Pa's previous statement, "Dogs don't learn anything tied to a chain or cooped up in a pen", Queenie hunted four or five days a week. Of course, Pa carefully screened the hunters who he let borrow our little beagle. One such lucky fellow was Ray Woolston, our school bus driver. Ray soon loved her as if she were his own. Naturally, everyone around Farwell soon knew that she was something special.

When Queenie was three years old Pa agreed to have her bred to the best male he could find, near at hand. I was too young to be let in on such things, so I never learned who owned the male. I do remember that she had six puppies and they were all spoken for before they were born. Pa wouldn't agree to any more litters, "It takes too much out of a hard-working dog." None of the pups were registered, which grieved me later in life, when I raised beagles. Queenie's known lineage ended with her death, in spite of an effort by my friend Archie and me. We attempted to breed Queenie and Spot, but it ended in failure. I guess our old female was just too old. You had to understand my dad and many others who thought that " papers never made any hound a better rabbit chaser."

When I was about seven years old my older brothers and Don let me tag along on rabbit hunts, "to carry the rabbits." I soon learned that when Queenie announced she had one up and running, Mr. Rabbit had better head for a hole or he would soon be rabbit stew. Most ended up in the latter category. At the end of the day our game pockets were always bulging with rabbits, partridge, and an occasional duck. Boys reared on farms knew how to handle shotguns and rifles and when one spoke, game was usually in the bag. We needed the meat.

Thanksgiving Day brought all the family together for a big feed. The meal was late in the day, as the morning and half the afternoon were devoted to rabbit hunting. In 1936, the deer herd had increased to the point where the Conservation Department allowed a "bucks only" hunting season from November 15 to 30. The Thanksgiving Day rabbit hunt then became the family deer hunt. Something special was lost, especially for me, as I wasn't old enough to hunt deer until 1939. It wasn't that rabbit hunting was forgotten, it was just because the deer season only lasted sixteen days and all hound owners felt uneasy running valuable dogs with the woods full of "city slickers." And so, the last half of November became the deer season and we hunted rabbits the rest of the time, from October 15 to January 31. Queenie didn't seem to mind taking the deer season off. Perhaps she even enjoyed the rest.

My older brother, Bernard, owned an old .410 Stevens (Model 44 1/2) shotgun. It was a single shot that broke open by moving a curved lever, located under the breech. It was clearly stamped "44-Shot", but we only shot the short two and one half-inch .410 shells in it. One day, just before the opening day of the small game season, Pa called me aside and handed me Bernard's old gun and a box of .410 shells in #6 chilled shot.

"Well, young man, I think you are old enough to go hunting," he said. "Here are the rules, and if I ever hear of you breaking any, there goes your privilege." I thought that this was the most important moment in my young life and I listened intently, as I wasn't about to break any rules. I was only ten years old.

"You can't hunt with anyone, not even your brothers. So if you shoot anyone it will be yourself. Always unload the gun before climbing fences. Don't ever carry a loaded gun into the house or barn. Don't ever point a gun at anything you don't want to kill. You already know a lot about guns and hunting, so I'm sure everything will go all right."

These were pretty powerful words for a young farm boy to hear. It meant that I could now get started harvesting those rabbits that meant so much to our winter-food supply. I never forgot the moment.

Queenie must have had some strange thoughts when a few

days later I let her out of the kennel and headed off for the back "forty", toting the little shotgun. I knew she would hunt for me. She would follow anyone with a gun, as she knew what was up. It was just getting daylight on the first day and if I timed it right I could get in an hour of hunting before the school bus came. Pa told me that he would pick Queenie up if she were running when I had to quit.

Going to school was my first job. No rabbits were bagged that first morning and hunting before the bus came just didn't work out. However, I found that I could get in an hour or so of hunting after getting home from school. This meant that I had to do my farm chores after dark with the aid of a kerosene lantern. Saturdays were different as I got the chores done early and headed out. If my parents worried about me they never let on. Most of the time they could hear Queenie running by just stepping out on the back porch. I didn't venture very far afield, as I didn't have to.

There were plenty of cottontails to chase right in our back-yard, so to speak. But after only a few unproductive hunts, Pa expanded my hunting territory to include all the land north of the Pere Marquette railroad tracks. "Don't cross the railroad, because that's big country and you aren't quite ready for that yet."

As there was a small cedar swamp on the north side of the tracks, I knew that the jackrabbits were now fair game and I set out to bag one. Habitat conditions for hares and partridge in and along these cedar swamps were ideal in those days. Deer were scarce and didn't yard here, so the cedar boughs grew clear down to the ground. I soon located a thick stand of ground hemlock in the western part of the swamp. It was a perfect place to jump a hare. I already recognized most tree species, especially the hemlocks. Jim and I had cut one by mistake for a Christmas tree one December.

"You two boys get back there in the swamp and cut a spruce or balsam, this one is a hemlock," Pa scolded. After packing that tree all the way to the house, we never made that mistake again. Ma liked big Christmas trees!

My hunting went on and on. Queenie did her part. I saw plenty of cottontails, all zipping past before I could get a bead on them. I hadn't yet learned that you just point a shotgun and pull the trigger. So here it was, the middle of December, and I still hadn't bagged a single rabbit. The hares were different. They simply headed off for the other end of the swamp and made little circles there until I moved over to where Queenie was running. Then the buggers would go back to where I had just left with Queenie in hot pursuit.

Finally, it happened. As I hurried off for the other end of the swamp, I crossed a small aspen ridge to get to where the little hound had been running for twenty minutes or so, and there under the butt end of a fallen tree sat a big snowshoe hare. I first spotted the rabbit's eye, standing out against the snowy background. With a careful aim at the rabbit's head, I bagged my first game animal.

Talk about excitement: a big white hare, a worthy trophy for a budding hunter, just ten years old.

CHAPTER FIVE

I N THE YEARS TO COME THE RABBITS FELL THICK AND FAST, ESPE-
cially after I found out that the best way to hunt was to
stand still somewhere near the spot where the rabbit was
started and wait for the rabbit to circle back. About the same
time I learned that you point shotguns and aim rifles.

When I was thirteen I started to hunt with my friend, Archie
Rogers, who was now allowed to hunt with Spot, the beagle that
lived a half mile east of us. Queenie and Spot made a good pair.
Queenie's chop voice didn't travel as far as Spot's loud bawl. We
soon started to concentrate on hunting the hares and the dogs
were usually within hearing, even when they headed off for the
other end of the swamp. This was true for all the swamps we
hunted, except for the big one, Deadman Swamp. And after the
first season of hunting together, that's where we headed.

Neither of us owned a good compass, but we each had one
that probably came in a Cracker Jack box. On cloudy days we
spent lots of anxious moments down in the middle of the big
swamp watching the little needles on those compasses go round

and round and then trying to guess which way was north, the way back to the railroad tracks. Fortunately, a lot of trains ran on the Pere Marquette in those days and by listening for trains and orienting by our little compasses we spent no nights in the big swamp.

It was common for other, much older hunters, to get lost in Deadman Swamp. The story of two such fellows even made national radio, "The News Comes to Life." They spent two days and two nights in the big swamp before walking out. The swamp was seven miles long and three miles wide at the widest part, with few natural landmarks in those days. However, Archie and I knew some of the swamp's secrets. We knew the small feeder streams that flowed into and out of Deadman Lake because we fished brook trout in them during the summer.

Also, we knew our way around Deadman Lake as we spent many days fishing panfish and bass in the lake. As we spent more time in the swamp we found a few aspen ridges and soon learned where they started and where we would end up if we stayed on high ground. We loved the excitement of the big swamp and had no fear of getting lost when we followed our little hounds deep in to the interior of the swamp.

When I was fifteen, I bought a used 16-gauge LeFever, double-barreled shotgun. However, I had already hunted with Pa's 12-gauge double-barreled with the exposed hammers. In fact, I bagged my first partridge at age thirteen, and numerous ducks with the big shotgun. So, a handy little 16 gauge really appealed to me. It was my pride and joy! The money for the new gun came from money earned by working for neighborhood farmers at a dollar per day. Archie and I were strong young boys and were sought out by local farmers, especially during haying.

Archie already had a 12-gauge double-barreled shotgun that
had belonged to his dad.

So now we set out to hunt pats and ducks in earnest. The
duck season opened early, one year on September 26. From
opening day until small game opened on October 15, we hunted ducks at every opportunity. We knew where every marsh,
pothole, or beaver pond was located within walking distance of
the farm and that was about three miles in all directions. No
duck dropping into these small water areas was safe when the
season was open. But when the small game season opened we
switched over to rabbits and partridge. So the routine became
shotguns for ducks, rabbits, and pats as long as the partridge
and duck season lasted. However, partridge season closed
November 7. Then I switched over to a .22 caliber rifle for rabbits.

I owned a Stevens visible-loading repeater. Most people
called them pump-guns. It loaded one small .22 cartridge each
time you racked the action. That is if the fired-shell casing did-
n't hang up in the barrel, which was a regular happening with
my old rifle. My brother-in-law, Don, solved my problem by
lending me his Model 74 Winchester, semi-automatic .22. Now
there was a real rifle. I practiced until I became pretty good with
it. Actually, I credit Archie's dad for giving me the inspiration to
become a good rifle shot. It was only a casual remark that old
Bill Rogers made that stuck with me. Mr. Rogers once knew a
guy who shot at gun shows and he told us all about how the
expert trained.

"You've got to shoot every day," the old man said. And as .22
shells were cheap, that's what I did. Small tin cans, old flashlight
batteries, even the bases of shotgun shells, littered our back

yard, all with .22 bullet holes in them. Pa had died when I was only thirteen and Ma said nothing about all the shooting.

When I first started hunting rabbits with the .22, my score wasn't so hot. But, with practice I soon became pretty good, and eventually I didn't feel handicapped when armed with a rifle.

I often bagged rabbits that would have been out of range of shotguns. The cottontails were the most difficult, but the snow-shoes were usually easy. Even when pushed by the little hounds the hares had a habit of stopping to check things out after every few jumps. "Crack" the little .22 rifle would bark out and usu-ally another hare would be available for the pot. Archie still car-ried his old double barrel. His father had improved the shot pat-tern by pounding the muzzles with a brass ball-pein hammer. At least we both believed it had helped. And Arch needed the help.

My reputation with the Winchester grew, mostly by Archie stretching the truth. I heard reports like, "The limit, all shot through the head." I knew better. I remember a lot of easy shots missed and quite a few rabbits were run down by the dogs after passing my stand. I still remember one big hare. I was standing on a tote road in the cedar swamp near Miller Lake. There was a small cedar bough on the ground just off my left foot. The dogs had given this hare a run for the money, way off to the north and now he was headed back and straight for the spot where I waited.

How he got there I never figured out but there he was, one big hop right behind the cedar bough, all of three feet from my left foot. At my shot the hare jumped about three feet straight up and lit off for the other end of the swamp. He didn't want anything to do with us. He crossed the Maple Grove Road and went clear out of hearing to the south. Archie and I gathered up our little hounds that evening, just as darkness fell.

Archie and I were inseparable. Spring, summer, fall, and winter we were in the woods, along the streams, or on the lakes. I always had chores to do on the farm, but Archie could be depended on to help out, especially on days we had something planned, and that was almost every day, except Sundays, which were reserved for the Lord's day. Both our families were deeply religious and we grew up going to church every Sunday.

I remember a major uproar caused by a preacher bagging a nice buck on the first day of the deer season, a Sunday. Reverend Teachout loved to hunt and who would know if he just went out a couple hours before church? He hadn't thought it through though. What would happen if he shot a buck? And that's what happened. Soon after that Archie and I started to hunt on Sunday, as our older brothers always did. Not one word of objection came from our parents. And our little hounds didn't care what day of the week it was.

We were still expected to go to church before setting out into the woods for the rabbits. The church was located one mile east of the farm on the south side of the road, next to a stand of sugar maple, for which the road was named, Maple Grove Road. It was called the Union Church, as it was non-denominational. Various preachers took turns delivering the Sunday service. My favorite was Charley Kleinhardt, who came from Brown Corners northeast of Clare. He always got his message across without losing his dignity.

Then there were those who preached fire and brimstone and the little church almost rattled with their yelling. Their supporters in attendance joined in with "Amen" and "Bless the

Lord" which I always thought added to the confusion of the moment. Then there was the music.

The church had an old organ that some gifted man kept tuned up so that it sounded pretty good, especially to my untrained ears. But the highlight of the worship service was when old George Liddell honored us with a violin solo. Mr. Liddell lived across the road from the church and didn't attend services every Sunday. So on the days he attended, we knew we were in for a special treat. His violin was a Stradivarius, and he always took the time to inform everyone that it was the genuine article. He said he got it in Canada when he served there with the Salvation Army. Anyway, it made beautiful music that calmed the souls after so much loud preaching.

CHAPTER SIX

ND SO IT WENT, THROUGH GRADE SCHOOL AND INTO HIGH school. Archie and I always fished and hunted small game together. However, we never hunted deer together. I always carried a special fascination for those big game animals. I often dreamed about the day I would bag my first buck. As I mentioned earlier, we had few deer around the farm when I was a youngster. I vividly recall the first deer I saw on the farm.

It had been a hard winter. The snow came early and stayed late. Now the alfalfa field behind the barn was showing bare ground with a few green spots here and there. My mother who had been out feeding the chickens and gathering eggs suddenly returned to the house.

"There are two deer out in the hay field behind the barn," she excitedly announced.

Pa, who had been getting the milk pails and ten gallon cans ready for the evening chores, and we three youngsters, the only ones still remaining home from the ten kids, all rushed out to the barn to see the deer. Meanwhile, Ma cranked the party-line telephone hanging on the dining room wall. She had to tell the Finch family across the road about the deer. Soon there were seven of us out there by the barn, watching the deer feeding in the hay field over a quarter of a mile away. The year was 1932 and we lived in southern Clare County.

My two older brothers and brother-in-law, Don, knew that a few deer had wintered in Deadman Swamp and that several deer had yarded in some of the larger cedar swamps in northern Clare County. But when we saw the deer in our hay field it was really big news. Don told stories about hunting down the few scattered deer when he and his boyhood friends ran across deer tracks while they were rabbit hunting near Lake George in the early 1920's. The rabbits were put on hold while Don and his friends went after bigger game. I could be counted on to listen to these tales with rapt attention as I could hardly wait to pick up a gun and go after the white-tailed deer. As it turned out, Don and my oldest brother, Bernard, were my chief mentors. I learned my lessons well.

Deer increased rapidly in our part of the state soon after we saw the first ones in our hay field. In 1936, a "bucks only" deer season was allowed. I understand that the cedar swamps in the northern part of the county and some in Lake County, to the west, were badly browsed out before the season was opened. However, Deadman Swamp and all the smaller swamps in our area were in good condition with cedar growing clear down to the ground. That's one reason we had the excellent small game hunting around the farm.

Don and Lawrence Finch, who lived across the road, were among the first successful deer hunters. I remember the excitement when these young men returned home with their bucks draped over the front fenders of their cars. I guess it was only natural that I was badly bitten by the "deer hunting bug." Bernard got his first buck during the 1939 season, but once he broke the ice he was hard to match. Later, I considered him the luckiest deer hunter that ever lived. Bucks just sort of gravitated toward his stands. He even got some that were coming from the wrong direction, while taking his turn as a stander during our deer drives.

I started to hunt deer with Bernard and Don in 1939, when I was fourteen. I still have my first deer license. I shot my first deer, an eight pointer, in 1940. Bernard had put me on the stand and he posted up just over a little knoll from where I stood. Two years later, November 16, 1942, we both were hunting on the same stands. But, this time it was Bernard's turn. He got a beautiful ten-point buck that weighed 172 pounds, dressed out. This buck had the nicest rack that I have ever seen from our hunting area.

I bagged three bucks with 16-gauge slugs before being drafted into the Army in March 1944. I missed part of my senior year in high school and of course, the 1944 and 1945 deer seasons. Oh, how I missed them! Don and Bernard wrote me about "how they got their bucks" while I was gone. I'm not sure that helped me bear the pain. November 15, 1945 was the worst of all. I recall that was the day the government let the HAM radio operators back on the air, after being suspended during the war. I was still in service and in communications with the Military Police at Camp Haan, California. I tuned up a SCR 808, which was a super military two-way radio, and listened in on the ten-meter band. I picked up a guy coming in loud and clear, or "five by five" in military lingo. It was Ray Clementi, a radio engineer with the Michigan Department of Conservation, and broadcasting from Roscommon. I couldn't hear his west-coast friend; something to do with radio skip I guess. Nor did he answer my attempt to call him. I knew he wouldn't hear my transmission.

Anyway, Ray's conversation went like this: "Today is the first day of the deer season back here." Later, "There goes a couple bucks on a car now." Oh me! How I wished I were standing on my favorite Clare County pine stump!

Since then the good Lord has treated me very well. I haven't missed another November 15 watching it get daylight on the opening day of the firearm deer season. To me, this is really the magic time of hunting deer. Anticipation of a wide-antlered buck working along a runway toward my stand always keeps me alert and ready. Unlike some hunters, I never go to sleep on a deer stand. Thanks to the old camp-deer law and now the second buck license, I average about a buck a year. Some years I fail to get a deer, but the next year I might get two. It's the hunting recreation that counts.

It would be unacceptable to me to have my season end at 8 o'clock the first morning. I honestly believe that repeal of the second-buck license will only penalize the law-abiding hunter. A few years ago cancellation of the old camp-deer law, which permitted a group of four hunters hunting together to purchase a second buck tag, caused disruption in our hunting camp. Fortunately, it was re-established the following year thanks to the good work of Senator Kammer. Some of my friends kidded me by calling the new law the Kammer/Schofield Act. Yes, I made my views known!

Part II

Authors Note

I'VE TRIED TO MAKE PART ONE AS ACCURATE AS MY MEMORY allowed. If I offended anyone, either by failing to mention him or her, or by casting him or her in an unfavorable light, I'm sorry. As noted, Part One was written in the first person form. Now as I lead into Part Two, which is fiction, I am changing over to the third person. The reason will become obvious as we proceed.

Why fiction, when so many stories remain in my memory bank? Well, I started this book soon after retiring in 1984. As I'm only a shade above a "hunt and peck" typist, my wife, Jeanne, helped me turn a rough, rough draft into a draft copy we could read and edit. As I reminisced about "the good old days" and put things down on paper, Jeanne kept asking me, "What are you going to do when I'm gone?" After several days of thinking about it, I decided to anticipate the future by writing Part Two as fiction. However, I've mixed in a liberal sprinkling of true recollections of years past. As you will see my mind got carried away, but it was fun. Again, if I have offended anyone, I'm truly sorry. The leading characters are real people who played important roles in my life, in the past and I hope, in the future.

Jeanne and I had the whole book down on paper prior to her death on December 19, 1995. I accurately predicted her death, even before she got lung cancer. She and I both knew that many smokers would pay the penalty. She finally quit smoking, but it was too late. As a non-smoker it has been difficult for me to accept anyone's addiction to tobacco.

After Jeanne's death I waited two years before I was able to get back to the book. This time I have had help from my computer. What a wonderful gadget. I wish I understood it!

Well, here we go. I hope you enjoy what follows.

CHAPTER SEVEN

AFTER RAY'S SECOND WIFE DIED HE SPENT MORE AND MORE time "over home" as he called the area from Farwell to the west Clare County line. One day when he was driving past the old farm, which was always his practice when in the area, he noticed a sign along the road, "FOR SALE BY OWNER." Ray now seventy-two years old, wondered how many owners there had been since the 1940's. He pulled into a driveway, leading to an old house trailer standing about where the old cobblestone house had been. At his knock an old lady came to the door. Ray studied her face and knew that he should know her but said nothing except to inquire about the sign.

"You will have to ask the Farwell Bank, as they handle all my affairs", the old woman replied.

Ray thanked her and returned to his pickup and drove the four miles into town. After parking in the bank parking lot he entered the bank where the receptionist warmly greeted him. She then directed him to the bank president's office. Ray certainly was no stranger to the bank personnel as his oldest brother had helped build the bank into the thriving business that continued after his death.

"Sorry to hear about your wife," the banker said. "But how are you holding up?

"About as well as can be expected under the circumstances," Ray replied. He avoided mentioning his own health problems that were gradually adding up as the years went by. "I see the old farm is for sale," Ray added.

"Yes, Mrs. Coloskey asked us to handle her business some time ago, and I just put the sign up yesterday," the banker replied. "Are you interested?"

"Yes, I might be, especially if you can buy out those squatters on the east "forty"", Ray replied.

He knew he was making a statement about those that subdivided the North Country into little parcels, all in the name of profit. First, they buy a piece of land, build a cabin in the middle of it, refuse to cut a tree, and the have the nerve to complain about shrinking game populations.

"Really, Ray, I've been in that house and it's pretty nice," the banker said. "But let me work on it. I think the owners of that house also own the old Wilds' place."

"Good," Ray quickly stated. "If the price is right I'll take the whole thing; the old farm, the house and the small acreage there, and the Wilds' place, too."

He wanted to get rid of the mess where the Wilds' homestead had once stood. With his business finished he left the bank and drove the hundred miles to Pentwater on the backwoods roads, as had become his practice when he was thinking about important topics.

"It helps to clear your mind," he told his sons.

A few days later Ray got a phone call from Al Reiss from Reiss Real Estate in Farwell.

"I've got some good news," Al said. "Herb asked me to help him put together a deal for you involving the old farm and connecting property. He told me to tell you that he didn't think you would mind involving us as we are all family."

"No, that's fine with me," Ray replied. "I would have had to turn to you eventually anyway."

"Well," Al continued, "I picked up a listing for that ten acre parcel, including the house, and the eighty acres of vacant land to the east. I believe you call it the old Wilds' place. Then I talked to Herb, at the bank, and we will sell you the whole package; 200 acres of land and the white house on the hill for $140,000."

Ray quickly calculated in his head, "About $60,000 for the house and the land at $400 per acre." And to think that Pa could have paid off the mortgage on the old farm, 120 acres, when the buildings were in good shape for only $2,000. Ray still refused to think that the intruding house was worth anything, even though he was realistic by mentally appraising it at $60,000.

"Well, Al, the arrangement sounds OK to me," Ray said. "I think I can scrape up that much money, but will need a week or two lead time before the closing."

"Ray, the owners of the land to the east are named Smith and we were just lucky that they are getting along in years and were thinking of moving back to the city to be near their family and hospitals," Al added. "Also, I want you to know that there will be some closing costs. But, Reiss Realty will not be charging you any commission. It will be nice to have you back in our neighborhood again."

That statement took Ray by surprise, as he had left Farwell in March 1944, soon after getting his Greetings from President Roosevelt. Al wasn't even a glimmer in his daddy's eye then. However, he didn't confuse the issue by mentioning it.

"Al, you might try to negotiate a little with the Smiths. Try offering them about $10,000 less then your listing. Draw up my offer that way and send it over to Pentwater for my signature," Ray stated.

Al then knew that the deal was as well as complete.

Two days later the papers for his offer were in Ray's mailbox. They were quickly signed and returned that afternoon. Less than a week after Al's telephone call, the Smiths accepted the offer and the closing was scheduled for the following Monday at 9 am.

Ray's weekend prior to the big purchase was a busy one. Shortly after getting the telephone call from Reiss Real Estate scheduling the closing, Ray called his old friend Archie Rogers. Both were widowers now and had started to fish together again, after years of short visits. Archie didn't hunt anymore, as it just brought up memories of his brother Lew. Lew had taken Archie under his wing when their parents died. The brothers were very close and Ray understood when Archie always turned down his invitation to join him on a hunting trip. Ray knew that Archie had Lew's old Browning Sweet Sixteen shotgun, a beautiful firearm.

"Are you going to be home this weekend, Arch?" Ray asked.

"Sure come on up, I'm getting quite a few perch through the ice on Crystal Lake," Archie replied.

"Still got your shanty out?" Ray asked.

"Yes, you know I don't take the cold any better than you do," Archie replied.

"OK, I'll see you about ten tomorrow morning," Ray said.

"Just meet me at the shanty. You know where it is. I want to get on the lake a little early because that's when we're doing best," Archie added.

Ray was feeling pretty good about developments as he headed his pickup up the freeway at 7am the next morning. He was hoping that his old friend could be convinced to join him in this new venture. Ray knew that both men had reached the age when they needed someone close at hand and this would be the perfect opportunity to broach the subject with his old boyhood chum.

"There's just something about a nice, warm fish shanty to bring out the best in people," Ray thought. What a perfect place to make a deal with the unsuspecting Archie. Not that he had anything sinister in mind. It's just that Ray knew that Archie would need some convincing to agree to his plans. This would mean major adjustments by both men.

Saturday went well. The perch were biting and the men half filled a five-gallon drywall bucket before calling it quits.

"We don't want to stay up all night cleaning fish," Archie finally said.

Ray had spent most of the day keeping the conversation directed at the good old days when they were hunting snowshoe hares down in Deadman Swamp

"Yes, and we sure had fun fishing. Do you think we could catch any brook trout over there now?" Archie asked.

"Sure, I don't know why not. Let's give it a try next summer," Ray commented.

"I'd like to visit the old homestead again," Archie said as he took the bait Ray had put out.

Neither man said another word about the subject for the rest of the day.

Sunday morning found the old friends out in the fish shanty again. Some of Archie's young friends had come by Saturday night and helped clean the big catch of perch. He kept out ten nice perch for their supper and gave all the rest to his friends.

They were reluctant to take so many fish home, but Archie said, "We'll get more tomorrow."

Ray hoped the fishing would be a little slower today and he got his wish. Now they could talk about serious business. "Sorta' reminds me of the fishing through the ice for bluegills on Miller Lake, eh, Arch?" Ray said, as he kept the bait out for the big moment. Finally, Ray thought the time was right to discuss his plan. "You know, Arch, we're not getting any younger."

"Yes, I believe we are about seventy two now," Archie replied.

Ray already was but went on, "I don't believe I've told you, but I've got a chance to buy the old farm. It's just not the same down there on Pentwater Lake with Jeanne gone, and I'm thinking about moving back over to Farwell."

Archie remained quiet as he had thought about the same thing after losing his wife. Finally, he broke the silence. "I don't know Ray, I've always heard that you can't go back."

"Well, I'm pretty certain that I'm going to try and I want you to consider joining me," Ray stated. Both men remained silent for a few minutes, interrupted only by a couple bites with no fish hooked. It was obvious the men were letting Ray's comments sink in.

Finally, Ray started the conversation again, "I asked Reiss Real Estate to see if I could buy the old farm and they put together a package deal that includes the old Wilds' place, too."

Ray was pleased when Archie asked, "Isn't that your sister and brother-in law's real estate office?"

"Yes, but they are both gone now and their grandson is running the business," Ray answered. He knew that Archie understood that he was dealing with "family," so to speak.

"You know someone built a house down there on your east forty?" Archie asked.

"Yes," Ray replied. "Isn't that a crime?" Ray knew that Archie would be thinking about all the rabbits they had bagged out of that swale hole and the hillside to the east, where the house now sat. "I insisted that the house be part of the package. Want to come over when I burn it down?" Ray asked.

"I still haven't heard where I fit in. Are you planning for me to be the arsonist?" Archie jokingly asked. Both men had a good laugh out of that remark. Neither of the men had done a dishonest thing in their lives and they were certainly too old to start getting in trouble now. Just then a school of large perch came in and the little fishing rods bent over fast and furious for several minutes. "Hey, Ray, I think you had that dry spell all planned, so you could get out your plan," Archie shouted above the din of the excitement in the shanty. Finally the perch moved on and another dry spell set in. "Well, I'm waiting," Archie said. "What do you propose?"

"I'd like to have you go in with me and buy the Wilds' place. I know it's not your old homestead, but it's just over the fence," Ray stated hopefully.

Archie was visibly moved. If there was better light in the shanty, Ray might have been able to see the tear that ran down his cheek. Ray knew that money didn't present a problem to either man. Ray had made some money in a few real estate deals since he retired. Archie never did let any grass grow under his feet. Even now he had a couple deals going that promised pretty good profits.

Finally, Archie re-opened the conversation; "I've got some reservations, Ray. It's like this. We both have a little ornery streak in us. We were even that way when we were kids. But you were a couple months older and it always became my job to back down. It's not like that now and I'm sure we are pretty set in our ways." Ray didn't reply immediately as he knew Archie was right. Yet he honestly thought it would all work out.

The men sat silent for a long time. Fortunately another school of perch came along and things were pretty hectic for a few minutes. As Archie was reeling in a big perch he suddenly blurted out, "OK, let's do it."

Ray was jubilant, but didn't want to spoil the moment. "Good! Can you meet me at the Doherty Hotel for dinner tomorrow night?" Ray asked. "We'll stay over and work out the details Tuesday."

"Suits me, I'll be there about six o'clock" Arch replied.

"I'm meeting all the parties involved at the real estate office at ten o'clock. You can meet me there if you prefer, but it's just that I didn't want anyone to get scared off with the middle man idea." Ray explained.

"That's all right, it will be best if we meet at the hotel. Reiss Real Estate might want a big commission if they thought you were buying the property for me," Archie said. He knew that Ray would bring all the papers so that he could determine exactly what took place at the closing.

The day's fishing soon ended. Ray took all the fish home so he could give fresh perch to some of his Farwell relatives the next day. "They aren't going to get them cleaned this time," Ray told Archie. Ray's pickup had a special purr as he headed down the freeway late that afternoon. Everything had worked out according to plans. "Michigan sure has a wonderful highway system," he thought.

The next morning found him entering the real estate office right on time. He had followed that road so many times that the car seemed to be able to follow the road without much steering. Today he drove the Buick.

All parties arrived within a few minutes of each other and all sat down at a big walnut table where Al Reiss offered coffee all around. Ray thought about how far the business had progressed since his sister and brother-in-law had first opened an office fifty-one years earlier. He knew that his nephew, Hershel, Jr. and his wife, Ruth, had worked really hard to build the business after his sister and brother-in-law retired. Now it was Al's turn, as so often happens in a family business. Al introduced Ray to the group. A closing officer represented the bank, so Ray didn't know anyone in the room except Al. The Smiths were there and old Mrs. Colosky.

"So that's who she is," Ray thought, "I should have known."

"How are your folks," she asked. It was obvious that she was living in the past.

"Oh, they are fine," Ray politely replied. The bank-closing officer started the business at hand by stating that the bank had a power of attorney to conduct business for the Colosky family. He had asked the old lady to be present, as he thought if the woman could realize that the farm was being returned back to the Schofield family it might be easier to talk her in to entering the Clare Rest Home. All her family thought that would be best for all concerned. With Ray buying the farm it would be easier, and it was.

Ray waited for all to depart before telling Al that his work wasn't over. "Al, I've got another thing for you to handle, if you would be so kind," he said.

"Glad to help you out anytime, Ray," Al replied.

"Well, I have a partner in this transaction. I didn't bring it up until now, as I didn't want anything to get off the track. Now that I own all the property, I want you to draw up the papers to give him title to the Wilds' tract," Ray stated.

This caught Al completely off base, but he quickly recovered. That was a Reiss characteristic, being able to shift gears without a lot of fanfare. "I think I better check with my attorney to find out how to do that without a lot of extra expense," Al replied.

"Please phone him now, Al, as I want to have this cleared up today," Ray requested.

After a few minutes in his private office, Al returned and said, "Everything is set. You just sign a quit claim deed and we will draw up a warranty deed transferring the property directly from the Smiths to your partner." Ray knew that would do it and he suspected that Al did, too, but said nothing. The telephone call remained a mystery, but no one brought it up again.

"How much money are you getting for the eighty acres?" Al asked.

"Well, I figure I paid about $400 an acre for the vacant land. Perhaps the old farm is worth a little more than that, but the Wilds' place sure isn't. Figure it out at $25,000 even. That way everyone will come out OK," Ray replied.

"All right, I'll make out the papers that way, but who will the new owner be?" Al asked.

"Archie Rogers," Ray answered.

"And his address?"

"Maple Grove Road, Farwell, the same as my new address," Ray replied.

That night the two old friends did a little celebrating at the Doherty Hotel. Archie even had a cocktail before dinner. Ray had his customary two Manhattans. The food was excellent, as always.

"This has always been a first-class restaurant," Ray told Archie.

Archie knew that Ray should know. The way he heard it Ray practically lived here on weekends while attending Michigan State College (now University). He sometimes drove up for a night during the week, too. There must have been some attraction, and Archie knew that Ray's first wife came from Clare. That was a long time ago and neither man brought it up. They just didn't think much about women anymore, except for their warm memories of their second wives. Both had successful second marriages, after rocky first ones. Perhaps the fires that caused so much trouble the first time had died down a little, allowing them to better control emotions. Ray knew that was his situation, but he never really knew about Archie. Even when they were boyhood friends women weren't discussed. Of course, then it was "dogs, hunting, and fishing." Both hoped it would be the same again.

Both slept well that night and the next morning shortly before nine, they walked into the Reiss Real Estate Office. Al was already there, busy with paperwork spread out on his large desk.

"Al, this is my friend, Archie Rogers," Ray said after the men had crossed the lobby and entered Al's office. "We grew up together on Maple Grove Road."

"Glad to know you, Archie," Al said. "I'd like to sit around and hear all about the good old days, but I have another appointment at ten o'clock and I want to get this business cleaned up before then."

With that, the paper signing began and at ten the men were parked along the Maple Grove Road looking over their new estate. Both were full of the excitement of the moment.

The first stop was on what they called the Clay Hill, located between the Wilds' place and the old Schofield farm. Ray walked along the road and watched the ground. Archie knew, he was looking for deer tracks. Sure enough, there they were, crossing the road just east of the house nestled in the trees. Perhaps a little farther east than in the old days. Probably the influence of the house, intruding on their normal movements. They soon found another deer trail crossing the road west of the house. Ray knew where it led.

First it skirted the big bog on the Finch place to the north and then crossed the road and entered the small swale on the Schofield east "forty". In the old days, before the house was built, the deer followed the swale margin on the east side. But now the deer obviously were avoiding the house by entering the heavy cover offered by the swale. Ray didn't miss a thing and filed the information away in his brain for future recall.

"Both these lowland areas look a lot smaller than what I remembered, eh, Arch?" Ray questioned.

"Yes, and we were a lot smaller then, too," Archie replied, and added, "you're still nuts about those white-tailed deer, aren't you?"

"Yes, I always said that November 15 to the 30, (the firearm deer season) should be declared a state holiday." Ray stated.

"The way I hear it you never did much else then, anyway," Archie said.

Ray accepted Archie's comments as being fairly accurate. After all, deer hunting revenues had fed his family and paid his salary during his long career as a wildlife biologist.

"Yes, I owe a lot to the deer herd and I've made a vow to spend the rest of my life protecting deer habitat," Ray told Archie with some emotion showing through. This he did by serving on the Board of Trustees of the Michigan Conservation Foundation (MCF), being a past president of the organization. (Editor's note: We have reprinted some of Ray's articles from the Conservator, the house publication of MCF, and included them in the Appendix.)

"When are we going to burn the house down?" Archie asked, as they moved down the road directly in front of the place.

"You know, that house looks like it is pretty well construct-ed. Maybe we ought to just move in," Ray replied. He was real-ly baiting Archie to see his reaction.

"No, I'm going to try to buy my old home site, remove the trailer house, and build myself a nice log cabin there," Archie said.

"You might think about building on that nice level spot, just east of my new house," Ray suggested.

And as usual, Ray was thinking ahead. It wouldn't be too many years before the old men ought to be living closer to each other. Besides, if Archie built there next to Ray's house, the deer would quit cutting across that corner and most could be divert-ed to the west of the house along the little swale hole, especially with a little habitat management that Ray had in mind. He knew that the first day of the deer season most of the deer traffic would be in a southerly direction, toward Deadman Swamp. You've got to plan ahead, and Ray knew exactly what was needed even though he hadn't been on the property for over fifty years.

However, Ray had been on the old railroad tracks about fifteen years earlier. The deer were still using the crossing on the east end of the big cut, the name the grade school chums called the railroad grade, just a half mile south of the old farm. The railroad grade and surrounding land were now in state ownership, being managed primarily for wildlife. Both old men felt pretty happy about that. It met their priorities. Besides, Deadman Lake would always remain undeveloped.

The railroad-crossing site wasn't exactly what you might consider a normal deer runway, considering the lay of the land. The old grade caused a backup of water on the north side, which the deer never crossed. The area east of the pond was too open and didn't give deer enough cover for safety. Ray knew that most of the deer coming from the north would skirt the west edge of a lowland conifer swamp, about a quarter of a mile north of where the tracks had been, cross over an aspen ridge and hit the grade exactly on the crossing. They had been doing it for as long as Ray could remember.

He remembered when the railroad section workers would burn all the right-of-way every spring. Actually, they just set it on fire and let it burn. Naturally, these fires produced excellent game food and cover. The small ridge was game cover at its best! Ray suspected that the ridge would now need to be cut over to restore the habitat, but that was not part of his ownership. Perhaps he could talk the state game managers into doing what he knew would help out with his long-range plans. But for now, he had to content himself in developing a deer ambush that would put venison on the table every November.

The old men discussed these things and a lot of others before Archie said goodbye and left for Benzonia. Ray knew a lot of work faced them and shortly after the Smiths vacated the house, he got busy. The wildlife habitat-management work had to be put on the back burner.

The Smiths had left the house in immaculate condition, he noted shortly after entering the house for the first time. Ray now knew that this would be his home for the rest of his life. He had felt the same way before with the Pentwater Lake place, but things change over the years. First he drove to Clare and went into Graham's Furniture. George Graham had grown up in the same neighborhood with Archie and Ray. He was a little younger and at that age a few months meant quite a lot, so the two chums didn't include George in their day by day activities.

George died young, but his store was still run by the family. Ray learned that one of his granddaughters had taken up home decorating and that is exactly what he had in mind when he entered the store. Not one to put off decisions, Ray handed her the keys to his new house.

"Please take a look and decide what's needed. My only guidance is to ask you to furnish the place with the best brands of furniture. I looked the place over and am very satisfied with paint schemes and everything has a fresh scrubbed look, so I don't think you will have to have anything repainted."

"OK, we probably can start on the project next Monday, if that meets your approval," she said. Then she quickly added,

"We can have a grand opening, so to speak, and if anything fails to meet your approval we will be happy to shift things around until they do."

Ray was busy looking at the young woman's dark eyes and coal-black hair.

"Just like her grandmother, Betty," he thought.

He almost missed the woman's question, "Do you have a budget to suggest, or maybe I should call you with my ideas after looking the place over."

"That's a good idea," Ray answered. "And if you're worried about my credit, I think your grandmother will vouch for me." Ray relieved her mind when he added, "Just do the job and bill me as you need funds."

Ray's mind was on Betty Loker when he left the store. "Maybe Archie and I spent too much time hunting and fishing," he thought.

Shortly after arriving home on Pentwater Lake, he called his favorite real estate broker in Pentwater. "I've decided to move back to my old stomping grounds, so I want to put everything here up for sale. That includes the house, the boat, my floating steel dock, in other words, the works," Ray stated.

"All right, Ray, I'll be over tonight and we can work out the listing," the Realtor answered.

Ray knew that he might as well start packing, as people were lined up waiting to buy lakefront property on Pentwater Lake, because a channel led out from the lake into Lake Michigan.

Ray often told friends that he could untie his boat and go anywhere in the world, "Right from my front yard."

Jeanne would correct him by stating that it was the back yard, as the front yard fronted on the street.

The Pentwater Lake channel is subjected to strong Lake Michigan currents caused by high winds. Consequently, sand fills up the harbor entrance. This requires annual dredging in early spring. Ray thought about the fifteen-year debate, who will pay for this year's dredging? Local folks were always upset with federal authorities that made decisions regarding channels to dredge based on tons of commercial trade shipped out of each port.

Of course, Pentwater is a recreation-based port and always ended up on the bottom of a commercial-based evaluation. This always rankled Ray. However, political pressure on the Michigan delegation in Congress managed to keep the channel open. People usually get more emotionally involved in factors that affect leisure time activities. Ray learned this early in his career when he was involved in "the deer wars."

Night after night he had to attend meetings and present reasons for harvesting antlerless deer. This was after working all day on other problems. Often these young wildlife biologists were shouted at and called stupid by men who never got out in the woods in the winter. Some even called Ray "that Lansing Office Biologist" as he had spent a few years there learning about budgets, personnel management, legislation, and other things that one needed to know in order to keep the biological arm of the organization going.

Sure, it hurt. But he soon developed a thick skin. He learned how to cope from the Master himself, the Chief of the Game Division. "Don't ever get angry at your opposition, or you will lose the debate," the big man told Ray.

In less than a week the Pentwater property was sold. Ray agreed to give possession to the new owners in thirty days, enough time to be sure that Graham Furniture would be through with their work.

"That's the way to move," Ray thought, as he loaded some personal effects in his pickup and headed east. A truck full of stuff would follow at a later date, but for now he was anxious to get in his newly decorated house. His son Randy, who lived near Ludington, had agreed to keep his pike-spearing shanty until it was needed.

"I sold the Pentwater house furnished, so how is it that I have some much personal gear?" Ray thought as he steered his little truck down US 10. Over the years, he always thought the same thing during his numerous moves and vowed to never do it again. But here he was doing it again.

"This will be the last time," he knew.

Randy, Ray's number two son, was a licensed builder and had helped remodel the Pentwater cottage into the comfortable home that was now being vacated. He thought that his dad had flipped out, but he knew it was useless to argue the point, so remained silent. He knew that his father didn't have many years left and no matter what, the old man wouldn't lose any money on real estate. Ray's other three sons all had different viewpoints, but accepted the fact that it would be a reality.

John even told his dad, "Have fun. Spend all your money. Don't worry about our inheritance. Nobody left you any money!" Ray often wondered how four boys, born to the same mother and father, could be so different. Yet, he realized that the same thing was true in his own case, as he was the youngest of four boys born to his mother and father. However, Ray had six sisters to give the family a little balance.

If Ray left anything to his sons it would be self-reliance. "No one is going to give you anything in this world. You will get what you earn!"

After Ray had been settled comfortably in his new residence, he phoned Archie.

"Well I'm here Arch. When are you coming over?" he asked.

"I guess I could come over this weekend, if that would work into your plans," Archie replied.

"OK, see you in time for supper Friday night. We'll probably eat out that night, but plan to eat all other meals here. This old deer camp cook can still lay out a pretty good spread," Ray replied.

Ray was full of all kinds of questions, but that could wait. Archie had come this far and he didn't want to be too pushy.

About four o'clock Friday afternoon Archie rolled into the yard.

"Hey, this is quite a place," he said as Ray showed him around the house. Graham's Furniture had done a wonderful job furnishing the house, just the way the old conservative man had desired.

Obviously, it pleased both men. "Let's have a drink on it," Ray suggested.

"No thanks, but I'll have one with you at supper time,"Archie replied. This sharply limited the eating places, Ray thought, because only a few in the area served cocktails. Ray knew they would go back to the Doherty Hotel. Not a bad choice.

"Put your things in that back bedroom and make yourself at home, we've got a lot of things to do," Ray told his old friend.

After Archie had settled down in his room, the men left the house and walked out in the yard. It was a nice sunny day on the fifth of May. Every thing had that nice sweet promise of warmer days to come. The trees were leafing out and the birds were busy nesting and the males were still singing their heads off, just showing off for their mates. Across the road, on the east side of the leatherleaf bog on the old Finch place, a ruffed grouse was drumming. You have to hear one to appreciate it. It starts with a "thump, thump, thump," and ends with the thumps coming so close together that you can't count them.

"Isn't that great?" Arch stated. "He didn't take long to welcome you home."

The men walked out to the road and turned east toward the old Rogers homestead. Ray thought that would get Archie talking about his plans for the eighty acres.

"It doesn't look like I will be able to buy that five acres where our old house sat, as old Mrs. Thrush lives in a trailer there now," he finally offered. "So, this is where you think I should build my cabin?" as he gestured toward the flat ground on the south side of the road.

"Let's take a closer look at the site," Ray said. Everything worked out as Ray had hoped.

Archie finally said, "This looks like a good place to build, Ray, but just don't you tell the poor guy who has to dig the basement what lies under this fine layer of sand."

"Yes, we didn't call this Clay Hill for no reason," Ray added.

Both men were sure that a clay hardpan layer could be found just under the surface. Ray thought about the Michigan basement under his old home as the men continued to walk toward the east. The house rested over the basement, simply dug into solid clay about six feet deep. No concrete needed and the walls never caved in.

When the men reached the old Wilds' homestead Archie commented, "I don't think I ever saw such a mess, and to think that it's all mine."

The old buildings, never in good repair, had rotted and fallen in. As is the case with most abandoned homesteads, other assorted junk littered the site

"Now that I've decided that I won't build here, I guess I'll just hire a bulldozer to dig a big hole and push everything into it and cover it up," Archie said.

"The environmental protection folks will have a fit, Arch, but this meets the old adage, it's better to seek forgiveness than permission," Ray stated. "What's the difference whether the stuff rots away on top of the ground or six feet under?"

And as Archie had planned, on the following Wednesday two big trucks hauling lowboy trailers roared up Maple Grove Road. One carried a large bulldozer and the other a big backhoe. The dozer was unloaded down over the hill, by the remains of the Wilds' homestead. The backhoe, when unloaded on Archie's new home site, promptly got to work digging the basement.

"Arch sure doesn't believe in wasting time," Ray thought.

Both men had spent most of the weekend running levels and staking out the building site, so they were ready for the heavy equipment. They had a good laugh when one of them commented that they could now take care of each other in their old age.

Ray did wonder how Archie got the necessary building permits in what must have been record time, but didn't give it a second thought as he had business of his own to attend to. First thing on the docket was the preparation of a detailed wildlife plan for the old farm. Ray knew he didn't have many years left, so he didn't want to waste a single growing season. He didn't want to do the plan piecemeal, as he planned to have the old place used as a demonstration area to show young college students what could be done to restore wildlife populations on depleted farm soils.

The environmental movement had been good, but it had gone too far on some fronts. It bothered him to hear environmentalists promote the old ideas "plant trees, plant trees, don't cut them, and certainly no clear cutting."

Ray always labeled such people "pseudo-environmentalists." He knew that to have large game populations you had to maintain at least 35 percent of the managed tracts in the low-growth stages. He was even bothered by the move toward ecosystem management. To him it appeared that this movement wanted to restore everything to the original forest. This would mean that the old farm would be covered 100 percent by a white and red pine forest.

Certainly there would be no room for game management here. Diversity, he preached is always better for most all species of wildlife, both game and nongame. He was proud that he had played a role in creating the nongame program, even testifying before Congress to help get the necessary legislation passed. He was pleased that professional wildlifers were now directing the endangered species program, saving many species from extinction. Here again, he had to draw many eager folks in line when they blamed hunting for all the troubles.

"Sport hunting never was an important factor. Look at destruction of habitat as the culprit in almost all cases," he preached.

As United States turned more and more urban, his job

became much more difficult. Kids raised in cities just don't understand the complex relationships between wildlife and its habitat. He and Archie were fortunate to have observed these things firsthand as they grew up. It would help if all young folks had to grow and kill the food they ate for a few years.

He recalled a Ph.D. botanist telling a vegetarian, "At least I don't eat my food alive, as you do!" You have to think about that one for a few minutes before it sinks in.

CHAPTER EIGHT

NOW RAY SET TO WORK IN EARNEST TO DEVELOP THE OLD
farm into a model wildlife area.

Early summer would be spent in planning and perhaps some
of the work could be started by late August.

"Perhaps a rye field or two," he thought. He knew he was
thinking about attracting a few deer off the state land in order
to put one or two into the deep freeze. "That's not all bad," he
rationalized.

Archie's house building went as scheduled. The deer
responded as Ray had thought. He noted that they were using
the runway on the west side of the house with more frequency
even though summer deer movements were at a minimum.
Ray's son, John, knew some guy in Lansing with one of those
big tree movers. Ray hired them to move some spruce trees and
plant them on the west side of the house for a windbreak. He
had found just the trees he wanted in an old Christmas tree
plantation. The trees were ten feet tall and had never been

trimmed or cared for. You just can't grow trees for market that way and Ray got them for nothing.

"Plant them in a north/south line, close enough together so that their lower branches touch," Ray told John.

The trees went in all the way from the road to 150 yards to the south. John knew the old man had something in mind when he asked, "Why do you need such a long windbreak, Dad?"

"Never mind, I'll show you this fall," Ray replied. John then knew it had something to do with deer, as that's all Ray thought about in the fall.

The windbreak worked exactly as planned. It sheltered the deer runway on the west side of the house and soon the deer hardly knew the intrusion caused by the house was there. Deer tracks skirting the edge of the little swale picked up sharply because of two things: Archie's house and Ray's spruce windbreak. Now John knew why his dad wanted such large trees transplanted. He obviously thought he didn't have many years to wait for them to grow.

Next, Ray gave the old house trailer on his homestead site to one of Mrs. Coloskey's grandsons.

"Just get it off the place right away," he instructed.

In only two days the trailer was gone and the site cleaned up. Although pleased with the job, Ray wanted all signs of his birthplace eliminated.

He brought back the bulldozer and told the operator, "Push everything into that big hole where the old barn had stood and then level everything off."

When it was all done he seeded the entire area with a grass and clover mixture that he had used on the game areas in the Thumb fifty years earlier. Only old Marvin Cooley remembered the exact mixture. It was a wet summer and Ray's plantings, the trees and the clover patch, did very well.

Wild ducks nested on several potholes in the vicinity. Because of favorable water levels, they were successful in bringing off large broods of ducklings. He and Archie knew every wetland area within walking distance of the old farm. Ray watched the little ducks grow.

"It seems they are just small balls of down one week and then are growing wing feathers only a few weeks later," he thought.

One afternoon while he and Archie were having a cookout in Ray's backyard, he suggested that perhaps they should harvest a few of the surplus ducks come fall. He got no response from Archie. Ray wondered why he quit hunting ducks when the Feds forced the states to establish steel shot regulations several years ago. He didn't oppose the regulations, as he knew that lead poisoning killed thousands of waterfowl each year.

However, Ray always thought that hunters should be able to hunt geese in the fields with the more effective lead shot, but said nothing. He knew that the waterfowl biologists had enough problems without him stirring up more. And everyone knew the old man knew how to do that, especially for a good cause.

By late summer the wildlife plan was finished. He hired a local farmer to work up the old hay field, located over a quarter mile southwest of his new home, and seed it down to rye. The rye would be heavily used by deer this fall and then could be turned down for green manure next June. The soil needed building up, but Ray's long-range plan called for keeping that twelve-acre field permanently in rye for deer pasture. A lot of invading brush had to be removed to create the field and the young farmer who Ray had hired thought the old man was a little nuts to spend so much on the project.

No one except Archie knew exactly what was in the back of the old man's head. Sure, the rye field would attract deer but it would also create a large open field that would have to be avoided by the deer as they moved through the area on their way to the safety of the big swamp when the shooting started on the first day of the firearm season.

Ray knew that a lot of deer would be in oaks on the gentle rolling hills north of his place. As hunting pressure caused them to seek better shelter, they would move south along the east side of the big leatherleaf bog on the old Finch Place and cross Maple Grove Road along the west side of Ray's windbreak and then head off for Deadman Swamp.

Just south of Ray's house the old farm field had grown up to briars, sumac, thornapple, and other valuable wildlife food plants. Some of the latter were autumn olive, noted for spreading all over the landscape. Yet, enough small areas remained open to make the old field an almost perfect wildlife haven. Ray planned no changes on this acreage. He knew the deer would cross the semi-open field and enter the aspen stand to the south about where an old apple tree grew in the fencerow when he and Archie were kids and chased rabbits there.

Ray's long experience with deer helped him formulate a plan for intercepting them and perhaps turning a few of them into venison to help with the winter's food supply. He knew they would now continue south along the east side of his rye field until they reached a small lowland brush area about a quarter mile further to the south, follow the west edge of the wetland, and finally come out on an aspen ridge just north of the railroad grade. They would cross the grade on their historic crossing and then be in the safety of the big swamp.

As he mulled it all over he kept thinking, "The best laid plans of mice and men. An old white-tailed buck could make fools out of us all. That's why they are such worthy game animals."

Ray's plan for the big ambush was about complete, so he and Archie went to work building a permanent blind that Ray knew would be his last deer hunting spot.

"This is going to be a lot more comfortable then that duck blind on the beaver pond on the Deadman Lake outlet," Archie remarked as the men lugged white pine slabs off the few old stumps left in the area.

"Yes, it bothers me to have to build deer blinds. We used to get along fine by just sitting down next to a big oak tree. Or better yet, bagging your buck by still hunting," Ray replied.

Both men knew that the big increase in archery hunting had caused the deer to be much more wary on opening morning and if you weren't well-hidden chances are they would spot you right off. And, of course, Ray wouldn't admit that his age prohibited him from hunting like he used to in the good old days.

"Darned confound bows, lighted pin sights, and worst of all tree stands," he told Archie.

Archie knew Ray always called the compound bows by the more colorful adjective. Actually he accepted archers, as they bought licenses and cared deeply about the welfare of the whitetail, too.

As the blind neared completion, Ray lined it with burlap to keep out the cold north winds.

"Not too big or not too small," he remarked. "Too big and it will be drafty when the wind blows, as it usually does from

November 15 to 30. Too small and you won't be able to turn around to check out that deer sneaking around behind your back."

Ray remembered his old deer blind in Freeman Township. "Shot a lot of bucks there, Archie, but the blind was so small that a lot of them spooked when I moved to check on a noise coming from the other direction. And you never could figure which direction to watch."

"I'll be willing to bet that most of the deer will come from the north here," Archie remarked.

And of course that was Ray's plan.

"If I get here well before daylight, I might be able to get one leaving the rye field at daylight," Ray added.

As it was only September, the deer had plenty of time to get used to Ray's blind before November 15.

"Well, I'm ready Arch. Do you want to join me?" Ray asked. He knew the answer.

The men then returned to their home and checked up on Archie's construction project.

Archie's house construction had moved right along. He hired Schofield Builders out of Ludington. Ray's son, Randy, owned the company. Randy had worried about his dad moving back to the old farm and living all by himself, so he brought in some of his builder friends from Lansing to help get the job done on a fast track. Ray always thought it odd that so many boys from East Lansing High School had entered the building trade. Certainly, it had to be a tribute to a shop teacher who planted the seed.

Randy always said he inherited his skills from his grandfather who he never knew. Ray always bragged about his father's construction abilities. Anyway, the crew brought in a house trailer so they could live on the job site, and a big tool trailer equipped with a power generator so they wouldn't have to wait for the local electric company to install the necessary power. With all the conveniences of home the construction crew got right to work. Archie was much impressed.

Randy did the foundation and laid the blocks, as that was his favorite task. The other men pitched in and by Labor Day only the finishing touches remained. The house was a comfortable three-bedroom ranch, small but well constructed. Archie had given up on a log cabin when he found out how much maintenance was involved. Right after Labor Day the crew set about landscaping the yard.

"I want a few trees, but keep the yard small," Archie told the crew. "I don't want to spend my old age mowing and caring for a large lawn."

When all the painting was done he hired Graham Furniture to do the interior decorating.

"Something like Ray's, but with enough differences to make it stand out as not simply a copy."

He moved in on October 7, just before the duck season began. The pond, down over the hill south of the house, had ten or twelve mallards hanging around. Both old men noted their constant quacking and the morning and evening flights.

"Want to give it a try on opening day, just like the old days? Ray asked Archie.

"No, there's no way I'll shoot steel through that Sweet Sixteen Browning that I inherited from Lew," Archie replied. "If I ever hunt ducks again it will be with my 12-gauge double."

Both men were busy with other tasks and let the waterfowl season slip past, as usual. Ray always wondered why, but never came up with a valid reason. A lot of duck hunters just quit. Blame it on steel shot? Well maybe, but Ray knew that the popularity of duck hunting had been declining before steel regulations. Low bag limits and complex hunting regulations? Most likely, Ray thought, but these things could be expected with a declining resource base. You can't continue to drain wetlands without drastically affecting wildlife species tied to that habitat. Anyway, it was a good thing that deer hunting remained so popular. Deer hunting revenues financially supported a lion's share of conservation activities, including wetland preservation. Ray did a lot of griping about deer hunters getting the short end of the stick. But as long as deer populations remained near record levels, he didn't organize a formal protest.

Shortly after Labor Day Ray started to attend a lot of field trials for beagles. Mainly, he went to trials for the fifteen-inch hounds. Archie thought that something was up but didn't push the issue.

"I just like to hear the dogs run," he told his old rabbit hunting buddy.

As Archie was too busy getting his place in shape, he didn't have time to go along with Ray. And sure enough, shortly after Archie got moved, Ray drove into his yard with a beagle standing up on the front seat looking out to survey the surroundings. If you were a beagle field trial person, you would note that the hound measured fifteen and a half inches. Ray had watched his owner being frustrated by having him turned down as being too tall for the fifteen inch class. When he had earlier been accepted in trials, he always made it back for the second series. He even won a couple fun trials. Finally, right after the hound had been refused a place in a big trial, Ray approached the owner.

"I'll give you $200 for that hound," he offered.

"What are you going to do with a hound that you can't campaign, mister?" the man asked.

"I plan to use him on hares and he's exactly what I want, a loud chop voice and a hard-driving hound," Ray replied. "I've watched him run on some of the earlier trials."

"You just bought yourself a great hound," the man finally announced.

"I'm going to call him Rex. I think that was Finch's old dog's name," Ray told Archie.

Then he built Rex a nice, insulated doghouse and chained him to it with a long chain. Ray didn't like the arrangement, but he wanted the new hound to get used to his surroundings and be able to prove himself before building an elaborate dog run. He knew the main problem would be deer as they were everywhere. He recalled another well-bred beagle that resisted all attempts to cure him of the deer-running habit. Ray tried every trick at his disposal except the ultimate treatment that all hound men laughed about, but no one tried.

"First, you get a deer hide, including the legs and head. Put everything in a steel barrel with the unfortunate dog. Seal the barrel securely and the roll it down a steep hill."

Ray couldn't do that to his little hound, so he gave him to an old rabbit hunter who also failed to cure him. Finally the beagle was shipped off to southern Michigan, where few deer were found in those days.

After Rex had been with his new owner for a couple weeks, Ray started to take him afield on the old farm. He kept him on a leash until a rabbit was jumped. Then he turned him loose and followed closely behind to make sure he didn't leave the hot trail for a deer. Ray knew how to train dogs and managed to keep Rex off deer for over a month. When he finally started to let Rex search for rabbits on his own, he was pleasantly surprised to find Rex not the least bit interested in chasing deer. This is always a very satisfying moment for hound owners in deer territory.

During all this training Ray hadn't carried a gun. He made it a practice to shoot the .22 around the yard, especially when coming out to feed Rex. Here again, his worry was for naught. Rex learned to like firearms, as he expected a little attention from his master at times like these.

After Archie moved into his new house he would often awake early in the morning and hear Rex running rabbits around the swale southeast of his house. He knew Ray was down there, too, watching his new pupil develop into a first class rabbit hound. Archie would throw open the window and just listen to the hound music. It brought back wonderful memories of the good old days, when everyone lived a much more relaxed life.

Later in the day he asked Ray, "Wonder if he will ever be as good as Queenie?"

"No," Ray replied, "Queenie gets better every day."

No two hounds are the same. Ray planned that Rex would be the best snowshoe hare dog that he ever owned. Both men were disappointed that they couldn't find any hares in the little finger swamps north of the railroad grade. Deer had completely browsed out these cedar swamps, leaving nothing for the hares to eat or hide in. When you can stand on one swamp edge and see the aspen ridge on the other side, don't expect to find hares or any other kind of small game there. The old men knew that they could still find hares a mile east, down by Miller and Minnie Lakes, where they often hunted as boys. And, of course, across the tracks the big swamp had an adequate population. Ray didn't run Rex in either place yet. So day after day the cottontails around the old homestead got their legs stretched.

The rabbit season had been open since September 15, but no rabbits were shot. Finally, on October 20 Archie heard Ray's old .22 rifle crack once. He knew the men's diet would now include fried rabbit.

"Not many cottontails around, Arch," Ray later told his friend. "We've got to get busy with some habitat management."

Early one morning, about ten days after Ray had shot the nice, plump rabbit that he and Archie enjoyed eating for dinner, Ray looked out the kitchen window and saw a big cottontail in his back yard. Rex was in the house, so Ray let him out to give the bunny a chase. When he opened the door, down over the hill to the south went the rabbit, his cottontail flying. As Rex had been in the house all night, he had important things to attend to. When he finished, he started sniffing around and soon found the hot trail and the chase was on. The rabbit crossed the fencerow down by the duck pond and headed east toward the largest swale on Archie's "eighty". Around the swale went the rabbit with Rex in hot pursuit. The crisp morning air rang with hound music.

Archie came out on the back deck at his house and just listened. Suddenly the excitement of his youth came fleeting back. Just then the rabbit left the heavy cover of the swale and made a little swing to the south up on the side hill, now covered with briers, sumac, and scattered witch hazel. He found a clump of tall, dead grass and squatted down to watch for the pesky hound. Just as Rex reached the spot, the rabbit jumped up right in his face and headed off for the heavy cover offered by the swale. Archie saw the whole thing from his house. Ray, standing on the side hill just south of his house, knew that Rex was now enjoying a sight chase. Every rabbit hunter knows what that sounds like.

"That's a darn good hound," Ray thought, as Rex had no difficulty switching from a sight chase to the ground scent.

He knew that a lot of good beagles would still be sniffing around trying to pick up the trail. And a lot of rabbits run the dogs to a loss with this technique.

The chase went straight east through a couple small swales and clear over to the old orchard, just east of Archie's old homestead.

Both he and Ray had made friends with the old woman living in a house trailer on the site. She told her son, who drove out at least once a week to check up on her, all about the two old men "trying to relive their childhood." So Ray didn't worry about Rex running over there. He just stayed put, as he knew the rabbit would soon turn and come back on Archie's property, and it did.

"Rex is really driving that one," he thought with much satisfaction.

Suddenly a shotgun barked out, followed by Rex's silence a minute later. Ray instinctively knew, "Arch finally gave in. Now I've got my old hunting buddy back!"

Ray walked east toward the small swales on the east end of Archie's property. He soon found Archie with the dead rabbit swinging from his left hand with Rex prancing along trying to worry the cottontail. Lew Rogers' Sweet 16 was cradled over

Archie's right arm. Until then Ray had forgotten that Archie shot left-handed and his hunting buddy was grinning from ear to ear.

"I finally did it. Any dog that runs like that needs someone around to help him out and I knew you weren't going to do it."

With that, the men walked up across the fields to Archie's house. Their hunt done for the day.

After cleaning the rabbit and putting it in a pan of cold, salted water, Archie poured a couple cups of coffee.

Ray wanted to confirm Archie's return to the hunting clan, so said, "The weather report says that we might get a couple inches of snow tonight, so why don't we introduce Rex to the hares?"

"I haven't hunted jacks since we were kids, so I'm willing to give it a try," Archie replied.

"OK, I'll pick you up about 8 am and we'll try the swamp south of old Earl's place," Ray stated.

Both men knew that the swamp was only an extension north of the railroad grade from the big one. That's why it still had hares. This cedar lowland ran north of the tracks about three fourths of a mile, narrowed at the Maple Grove Road, and then widened to enclose both Miller and Minnie Lakes.

The weather forecast was right. It snowed about two inches during the night, the first significant snow of the season. Both old men were excited about the hunting prospects when Ray backed out of his garage with Rex sitting on the front seat beside him. Archie walked out to the road with the 16-gauge shotgun tucked in a case, as required by law.

"Where's your gun?" he asked.

"Well, I'm going to be the dog handler today, so all I brought is the Colt Woodsman .22. It's behind the seat," Ray answered.

Archie then knew that Ray didn't plan to bag any hares. He couldn't hit the broadside of a barn with a handgun. Never could.

"How can a guy be so good with a shotgun or rifle and be such a terrible shot with a handgun?" Archie thought.

It was only a mile down the road to the swamp they were planning to hunt. Both men knew why they drove the pickup. Never did it before, they were thinking.

"Remember when we slipped and slid down the road to hunt here, Arch?" Ray asked.

"Yes, school had closed because of the icy roads, so we went hunting, as usual," Archie replied.

They were now at the swamp and parked the truck on a wide spot in the road on the south side.

After getting out of the truck and getting organized for the big moment, Archie continued, "We had a pretty good day, in spite of the sleet storm. You stood over there on that little aspen ridge, just off the road and shot three rabbits before moving. Queenie chased them and you shot them, which was the way it usually went."

"No, Arch. I recall you did pretty well after your dad opened up the choke on that old double barrel. But there sure were a lot of hares in those days. The deer herd is great, but they sure have ruined our swamps," Ray commented.

"What's the plan?" Archie asked.

"Let's start over there on that little knoll you were talking about," Ray replied as he strapped on the Colt Woodsman and put Rex on a leash. "I plan to keep the dog on a lead until we get one up."

Archie knew that Ray was worrying about deer, as they certainly would run into some when they got into the swamp, but all signs pointed to Rex being deer-proof. Sure enough, a hare had crossed the little aspen stand during the night. Not much snow had fallen into the tracks, so the hunters knew that he wouldn't be far away. The trail crossed the ridge near the south end and both men knew that this was the place to stand in order to bag the hare when Rex got him going.

"Just like old times, Arch," Ray said as they looked down at the fresh snowshoe hare tracks.

The hind feet made tracks about twice as large as a cottontail's as he hopped across the small ridge.

"Why don't you stay here, Arch? I'll see if I can rout him out. But don't let him get away when he comes back," Ray added.

"You mean they are fair game on the first circle?" Archie asked, thinking back to when they shot more rabbits than they wanted to carry home so they made rules to make it more difficult.

"Yes, Arch, this is Rex's first hare and sometimes cottontail dogs need encouragement to switch over to hares," Ray answered, as he recalled other beagles that practically had to have hares waved in their faces before getting the idea that they were fair game to chase. Years ago his best hare hound had started out that way.

Ray hadn't followed the trail more than a couple hundred yards when the snowshoe jumped up from under a fallen cedar. Away he went in those long bounds for which the species is famous. But as so often happens he had to stop to look back to see who had disturbed his daytime sleep.

"That's why you guys are so easy for .22 rifles," Ray thought. They don't always do it, but it's common enough to wait them out if you're hunting with the little rifle. Even though Ray had the Colt Woodsman he just waited for the hare to take off. This one didn't take long before bounding off.

"Here Rex, here Rex. Let's get him!" Ray hollered to the beagle, trying to get his interest up.

The dog stuck his nose in the fresh tracks and looked up at Ray with a quizzical look on his face. "Hey boss, that's not a rabbit," he clearly indicated.

Ray kept following the hare, all the time trying to get Rex to take the trail.

"Nothing doing. I don't chase trash game," the little dog seemed to say.

Ray wasn't disappointed. He had seen it all before. After a short loop off to the south, the hare turned back toward Archie's stand. The 16-gauge thumped once and Rex's first hare lay dead in the snow. Ray hurried up the trail with Rex still trotting along behind wondering what all the excitement was all about. Ray was encouraged when Rex whined after getting a good whiff of hare scent. He knew he'd make a hare hound out of him yet. Ray made sure that Rex was on the trail when they approached the place where Archie waited. Archie wisely had left the hare lying in the snow for the dog to find. When Rex found the limp animal his tail wagged vigorously and he grabbed hold of the critter. With Ray on the hind legs and Rex on the ears, they danced around and celebrated. That's all it took. The old men then had a snowshoe hare dog.

"I saw another fresh track back there a ways," Ray told Archie. "Let's go back and see if we can get him up."

With that the men busted back into the thick swamp and in a few minutes had another hare up and running. This time when Ray let the dog go he needed no encouragement. The swamp soon was filled with his clear chop voice.

"Not yet with the clear enthusiasm of a cottontail chase, but that will come," Ray told his old hunting friend. "Let's go back to the road and let him run that one for awhile."

The hunters walked back to the road and just stood there and listened to Rex driving the hare. He first took him south toward the old railroad grade almost a half mile away.

"He must be almost to the railroad, " Archie commented.

"Yes, but the chase just turned and now he's coming back," Ray replied.

And back they came, the young hound giving the hare a run for his money. Ray smiled. It was obvious that Rex was enjoying his new found rabbit, one that laid an easy trail to follow instead of resorting to all those sneaky tricks of the cottontails. Hares relied on their long hind legs to put distance between themselves and those pesky dogs, or other enemies. Cottontails backtracked, jumped off to the side, and sometimes hid almost under the beagle's nose. Different rabbits, and different tactics.

"Thank God for putting them both here," Ray thought.

"That jack hasn't got much time to think things over, eh Ray?" Archie accurately observed.

"Yes, or to mess up his trail. A bigger hound drives rabbits a little faster and I like what I'm hearing," Ray replied. "I think he's going to cross the road."

Ray was glad that they stood in the road to watch for any cars that might come past. Both men wouldn't hesitate to flag them down, to save the dog. And cross the road he did, only about 20 yards west of where the men stood. Neither man made any effort to shoot the hare when it cleared the road in three or four big bounds as only hares can do. Rex was only thirty yards behind and in full cry.

"When he comes back, let's add him to the pot, Arch," Ray said.

"I think I'll go over to that little opening to the north and wait there," Archie said. "If he gets by me, it might be a long day. If you hurry you can get home and trade that handgun for a real firearm."

Ray knew that Archie was kidding him about being underarmed. Also, both men knew that catching Rex when he came back across the road would be an impossible task. Sixty years earlier Ray could do it, but not now. With that Archie moved off the road and crossed a fringe of lowland brush to the place where he would wait. Both knew it was there, although neither had seen it for over fifty years. Ray stood in the road with the Colt Woodsman in his hand, right where the hare and Rex had crossed.

The chase headed right for Miller Lake, just like the rabbits did in the old days. The hare made a small circle west of the lake and twenty minutes later you could hear Rex headed back for the road.

Archie was waiting in the right spot and when his shotgun roared out another hare was added to the bag. When he and Rex came back out on the road, the dog was grabbing for the rabbit on every step.

"We've got a real hare dog now, Archie," Ray said as he slipped the leash on Rex's collar.

"This is sure a different hunt then like in the old days," Archie thought. "It would be pitch dark before you could drag Ray out of the woods then."

Shortly after noon on the day following Rex's first hare hunt, the men had just finished lunch at Archie's.

With the second cup of coffee before them, Ray said, "My doctor tells me to lay off this stuff, but the old caffeine habit is pretty hard to let go."

"Yes, old habits die hard," Archie replied.

Both sat quiet for a few minutes and both knew what the other was thinking about. Archie and Ray blamed smoking for their wives premature deaths. They hoped that time would make some of the sadness disappear. It wouldn't.

"Here it is less than two weeks before the deer season and I'm training a new dog rather than out checking up on the deer," Ray said to break the silence. "Are you going to join me?"

"Not this fall, Ray. I've got to think about it for awhile," Archie replied.

Earlier in the day Ray had noted that Archie had purchased a senior's hunting license and he could hunt for almost all legal species, including deer. Now, he said nothing because he knew that Archie still thought of Lew every time he picked up a gun. Ray knew that he and Lew had hunted elk and mule deer together in Colorado, but Archie was never really into Michigan deer hunting as a boy.

"Think I'll walk out and check out the deer sign on my new rye field later this afternoon. I don't think it has snowed enough to discourage the deer from feeding in the field. Do you want to come along?" Ray asked.

When Archie indicated that he would go along the men made arrangements to leave the house about 4 pm in the hopes of seeing some deer. So a few minutes after four o'clock the old friends were hiking across the field behind Ray's house, heading for the rye field. As they approached from the north, both saw a couple deer leave the rye field with their white tails flying. Too far for old eyes to see antlers, but Ray knew both deer were does and were probably year old animals as neither were accompanied by fawns. The men walked out into the rye to check for sign. Deer tracks were everywhere in the soft soil and it was obvious that several deer had been feeding on the tender rye plants.

"And to think that we always called deer browsers, not grazers," Ray said. "Essentially that's true, but they love grasses, tender broad-leafed plants, and of course, farmers' crops."

As the men walked along the rye field near the east side and only about a quarter of a mile from Ray's new deer blind that they had built a few weeks earlier, they stopped to look at the tracks of an exceptional deer.

"Now there's one to write home about!" Ray said.

They didn't know it at the time but they had just made their acquaintance with the deer that they would later refer to as the "Big One." Both men hated to give names to animals except, of course, dogs. However, this deer rated something special and hence, the name. The Big One, on this his first visit to Ray's rye field, had spent almost an hour there. He did little feeding, as he was busy checking out the does. It was the peak of the rut and any big healthy buck had more important things to do than fill his belly. He was now a two-and-a-half-year-old buck and carried a wide spread eight-point rack. He was an exceptionally large bodied deer because of being reared on southern Michigan farms. And he carried the right genes. Ray noted, with a quickening of his pulse, that the big deer had left the field on a runway leading toward his blind. Neither Ray nor Archie knew what human emotions were in store for them, because of this deer, only four years from now.

With the rye field visit out of the way, the men returned to Archie's house and sat down for a meal of stewed rabbit that Archie had been cooking for most of the day. Here's the recipe:

STEWED RABBIT

Ingredients:

One rabbit (1 1/2 pound)   Two large potatoes
One large onion   Two carrots
One quart can tomatoes   Two celery stalks
One-half stick butter   One tsp. Salt
One-half cup parsley   One 14-$^{1}/2$ oz. can chicken broth
One cup of flour   One tsp. black pepper

Directions:

Cut up the rabbit and shake it in a paper sack with the flour and the above dry ingredients. Brown in a hot frying pan with the butter. Dice the potatoes, onion, celery, and carrots and put in a Crock-Pot. Add the tomatoes, chicken broth, and browned rabbit along with the juices created in the browning process. Lightly stir so that the rabbit is well coated. Cook on High for three hours. Reduce heat to Low and let simmer for two or three hours. The rabbit will fall off the bones. Let cool and carefully remove the bones. Reheat, stir up, and enjoy!

The meal was delicious and shortly after dinner Ray went home. He enjoyed an after dinner drink in front of his fireplace and then went to bed early, as was his custom. That night he dreamed about bagging the big buck on the first day. He really preferred bagging small bucks because they were much better eating. Here again, he had misjudged the big one's age. He thought he was at least three-and-a-half-years old. When Ray awoke the next morning, he was aware (deep down) that he really wanted to bag one more big buck. He knew that the buck in the rye field wouldn't quite qualify, at least this year. He thought about the one he shot on South Fox Island, 11 points, 196 pounds dressed. And then there was the one that came out of the orchards in Oceana County, twelve points with a wide spread.

He thought about the fruit farmers there who appreciated his help in thinning the deer numbers from their orchards. Besides the browsing damage on young tender trees, they especially don't like the big bucks that make buck rubs on the young fruit trees during the rut. He remembered standing in the corner of a new cherry orchard and counting a dozen new trees that were ruined by buck rubs. Fortunately, Ray's farmer friends loved to hunt deer and preferred to do the shooting during the firearm season.

"Tough work," Ray always said, "but someone has to do it."

Woe onto the conservative wildlife managers who sometimes refused to issue enough antlerless permits to do the job!

Yes, deer had a place in the scheme of things, but too many deer in the wrong places can be really troublesome. Ray thought about all the car-deer accidents and the resulting damage to automobiles. Yes, and even with loss of human life.

He remembered his arguments with the anti hunters. "What would you do with the southern Michigan deer herd?"

Here deer lived high on the hog. They have an exceptionally high reproductive rate because of their diet and relatively mild winters

"There is no alternative to hunting by the masses," he told everyone who would listen.

Because of Ray and many of his wildlife biologist friends, Michigan still enjoyed annual hunting seasons with one million hunters participating.

Ray was sure that the end of hunting wouldn't come in his lifetime, or even in the lifetime of his sons. But he worried about what might happen when practically all children would be reared in an urban environment and not be exposed to life in the wild as it really occurs. It's not a Disney World out there. It never bothered him to shoot deer. After all, he had observed mass deer starvation back before any herd management had been practiced.

"We had a terrible time selling deer population control," he thought.

His friend, Ilo Bartlett, was the state deer specialist. Bart never worked on another job and he dedicated his life to the white-tailed deer. He held the job from 1928 to 1964. It earned him a special place in Ray's memory. And to think the anti doe shooters even hung Bart in effigy on the lawn at the state capitol in 1959. Disgraceful.

The Game Division Chief was Harry Ruhl, a big man in more ways than one. He taught them how to debate the opposition.

"Never lose your temper in the heat of an argument. If you do, you will lose what support you might have in the audience."

Ray had no trouble following the Chief's advice. He was raised a "buck hunter" and understood the emotions of the opposition.

Ray had little trouble getting the message across. "You must balance the deer herd with the ability of the range to support it."

As a strong advocate of habitat management, he always tied herd control with a program to improve habitat for deer.

All this reminiscing on Ray's part took place as the old men trudged back toward their houses from the rye field. Ray had no idea about what Archie was thinking. Neither man said a word during their half-mile walk.

And then it was only: "See you tomorrow," as they each entered their comfortable homes.

Ray stoked up the fire in his fireplace insert.

"This is sure the way to enjoy a fireplace," he thought. "And to think that wood is free."

The little insert heated almost all of his house. He had a back-up gas furnace in the basement, but it seldom came on as long as Ray kept the fireplace going.

"Wood is a renewable resource and I burn little fossil fuel here," he told his friends. "Michigan grows twice as much wood fiber as it consumes."

Ray thought about the old conflicts between biologists, interested in more wildlife, and foresters, interested in growing more trees, especially red pines. He had a lot of personal friends in the forestry profession, so considered them "not all bad."

After a dinner of warm-ups, Ray turned to more serious things, like getting his gear ready for opening day. He had passed up his normal pre-dinner cocktail because he wanted to load up a box of ammunition for the deer season. This requires full concentration and as you get older you can't let your mind wander. And that has no place on the re-loading bench.

"Guess I'll use the .243 again this year," he thought as he sat down in the comfortable chair next to the reloading press.

He had set aside a special place in his den for this important task. The room was sort of a trophy room, without trophies. Lots of mementos hung on the wall and Ray liked to go in there to reminisce about the good old days.

"Let's see," he thought as referred to his reloading data. "45 grains of IMR 4831, in a R/P case, pushing a 105 grain Speer bullet, will produce a velocity of about 2,900 feet per second."

A very accurate and adequate load for deer if you point the

rifle right. Ray always went through this thought process, even though this was his standard load, to be shot in his favorite deer rifle. He had used the same rifle for over 20 years. Ray knew that the time was here to go back to the old .30-06 Springfield or perhaps his Browning A-Bolt in .308 caliber. Deer just don't go so far after being hit with these bigger bullets and his doctor had even suggested that he give up hunting. Certainly, chasing cripples at his age and health status would be out of the question. Even though Ray knew how to point a rifle, he had given up shooting at hard-running deer a few years back. His old heart continued to weaken and he knew that tracking down a wounded deer was out of the question.

The only trouble with the old Springfield was that it can punish you on the range. Ray always practiced before taking a rifle afield for deer. The .308 wasn't bad, and of course, he could always go back to the old .30-30. He bought that one, a Model 94 Winchester, a few days after getting out of the Army in June 1946. He could never go back to hunting deer with a shotgun again, after experiencing the long-range shooting accuracy of rifles he shot in service.

He was an expert rifleman with the old 03A3 Springfield, just like the one that now stood in his gun closet. The old Springfield rifle was a military arm that saw service in both World Wars. However, Ray's had been converted to a beautiful sporter. He did most of the stock work, but had relied on gunsmiths for the alterations on the barrel and action. Many bucks had fallen before this old rifle before Jeanne bought him the .243 after noticing Ray's bruised shoulder after a session on the range.

He put a Weaver K-4 scope on the new rifle.

"The fixed power scopes do everything asked of them," Ray thought, "and it's certainly easier to pick up deer on the lower powered glass."

Both the .30-06 and the .308 were equipped with 4-power Redfield scopes. Ray recalled the day he had to convert to scopes from open sights.

"The front bead simply got fuzzy," he told his hunting buddies.

It was a sad day when put aside his old Gamemaster .300 Savage, put a scope on the .30-06, and started to hunt with it. There isn't anything as fast as open sights, especially if that's the way you were trained. Ray's friends knew that no buck that came within a hundred yards of him would be safe, even when on the dead run.

"You just squint down the barrel, line the bead up on the deer, and pull the trigger," he taught his sons.

Of course, learning to really shoot a rifle is not that simple. It takes years of practice, practice, and practice.

Ray's first experience with a scope turned out to be a disaster. He was still-hunting in Emmet County in the early '60's when a spike horn came up out of a tag-alder thicket and ran right past him at about twenty yards. The buck was chasing a big doe and when Ray threw the rifle up, all he could see through the scope was hair. He couldn't tell which deer he had lined up, so the buck escaped. The next day he carried the old Remington .300 Savage. Learning to shoot a scope-sighted rifle could wait until next year.

Ray's oldest son had started to hunt deer with the .30-30 when he was fourteen years old. He didn't get a deer that first year, but at fifteen Rob knocked over a big UP whitetail at ninety yards with one shot. The big buck carried a widespread eight-point rack. Dad was very proud, especially after neighbors called the local newspaper and son, buck, and the old .30-30 made the front page.

All four of Ray's sons shot their first buck with the same old rifle. He never got to hunt with it again and that's why the Gamemaster .300 Savage joined the family arsenal. Until the boys left home he had a difficult time keeping enough deer rifles around. Andy, the youngest son, still has the .30-30.

"Now that Andy has a new deer rifle, a Ruger .270 Winchester, I wonder if I could borrow it back for next year's deer season?" Ray thought. "It has a peep sight on it and I just might be able to hit another buck with it. And with Archie being left-handed, he could shoot the little lever action with ease."

The latter thought was really the reason Ray wanted the rifle back. He still planned to recruit Archie into the deer hunting fraternity.

The next day Ray got out his deer hunting clothes and laid them out on the bed in the spare bedroom. He owned plenty of good, warm clothes. Even some from his working days when he had to spend day after day in the swamps of northern Michigan.

"They never made anything better than the old felts and four-buckle Arctics," Ray thought as he got out his pair of Sorels, the nearest thing to the old favorite foot covering for men who had to work in the woods in below zero temperatures.

He always wore the Sorels ice fishing and on the very cold days of the firearm deer season. During most of the deer season he wore his LL Bean rubber bottom pacs. He laid out both pairs of boots now, as his doctor had recently warned him about hunting in the cold weather.

"Maybe you should just go to Florida and forget about hunting this year," his doctor had told him.

Ray pretended not to hear, but this fall he added a new item to his deer hunting gear, a kerosene lantern. He had looked all over before finding one. It was just like the one he carried to the barn to do the milking when he was a kid. Now it would be used to heat the inside of his burlap-lined deer blind.

The next day Archie heard a rifle cracking over behind Ray's house. He knew Ray was practicing with his .243, so walked over. Ray had put a target up on the little hillside south of the house and was now busy checking the sights on the rifle. Archie arrived just as Ray returned with the target in hand.

"Looks like it's right on, Arch," Ray said as Archie approached.

With a glance at the target, Archie agreed. "I guess you haven't lost your touch," he said.

"Now let's get out the .308 or the .30-06 and you can practice up a little and then join me back there in the woods on opening day," Ray suggested.

"No, Ray," was Archie's only response.

On opening day, a good hour before daylight Ray was walking down the fence between his property and Archie's. He was dressed warmly, ready for the day's hunt. He carried the lantern and the .243 rifle. After continuing south, he reached a fallen tree in the fencerow. This marked the spot directly east of his new blind. Turning straight west in the darkness, he reached his blind in only a few minutes. Ray moved carefully along this his chosen route, so he wouldn't spook the deer out of the rye field to the west. He knew that with this being opening day at least a few deer would be feeding in the field. They probably would remain there until daylight, before seeking shelter for their daytime bedding. He hoped some would come past his blind.

Ray placed the lantern in one corner of the blind, loaded the rifle, and waited for daylight. The lantern made an eerie glow on the scene as the light in the east started to make faint outlines on the few clouds floating past.

"A slight southeast breeze," Ray thought, "perfect for Opening Day at this spot."

The old man felt a twinge of regret that fewer and fewer of the young men growing up today were not out here witnessing and participating in the excitement of the first day. He recalled other opening mornings and took time to thank God for being able to be here on this day.

Ray, being the ever-optimistic hunter, knew that the deer in his rye field would very likely pass his blind on the way to the lowland brush to the southeast. Also, any deer up on the oak ridges behind the old Finch Place would be along later, as the hunters stirred them up and they headed for the security of the big swamp. He felt confident that some of them would follow his prepared runway, west of his house. The temperature was only a degree or two below freezing, with a promise in the air of warming up after the sun got up. All things considered, everything was nearly perfect.

"Very nice for my return to the old stomping grounds," Ray thought. "And to think Archie said we couldn't return."

Ray couldn't know as he waited, but the Big One and a lesser buck were busy sparring for the attention of a sleek doe. The deer were near the south edge of the rye field, just over a quarter of a mile from where Ray patiently waited. The four pointer was really no threat to the much larger buck. It didn't make any difference. The doe wasn't receptive, as she had bred two weeks earlier. But the bucks were not easily discouraged. Finally, the smaller one gave up his challenge and followed a doe and two fawns that were just leaving the field as dawn broke on the eastern horizon. The sleek doe and the Big One left the field on the south side and set off for the big swamp on an easy lope. They would be in heavy cover only a few minutes after daylight.

They soon crossed the old railroad grade only sixty yards west of a young hunter, guarding the crossing that was so heavily used by deer. The young man had wanted to make sure that no one beat him to this spot, so had been there for two hours already. He had paid the price for arriving so early and was now chilled clear through. Someday he would make a great hunter, but unfortunately he spent too much time looking east. The big buck and the doe got the young hunters scent and crossed the grade in big bounds with their white tails flying in the slight southeast breeze. They were within easy rifle shot of the hunter and running hard when the young man heard the brush cracking and turned to see only tails as the deer disappeared into the heavy cover. Both the deer and the hunter learned a lesson. The Big One's being that he had to get back to the swamp before daylight. He didn't forget it for the remainder of the season. Like his first season with antlers, he again got through the season without a single shot being fired at him. Deadman Swamp was a perfect hiding place for wary deer.

Meanwhile Ray waited in his blind. The lantern kept him toasty warm. With the first streaks of dawn came the first rifle fire of the new season.

"Same thing every season," Ray thought. "Some shots before it's safe to shoot."

Changes in the legal shooting hours wouldn't help. Most hunters with a buck in their sights can't resist. Like many hunting laws, only the law-abiding hunter would be penalized. Ray remembered one buck he let go opening day. The deer crossed only twenty yards from his blind. Even though it was legal shooting hours and he knew the deer was a buck, he let him go. He hadn't been sure about his antlers. The deer entered the cedars east of Ray's blind and obligingly waited for daylight. Then he came back out of the heavy cover and Ray added him to his long list of bucks bagged.

Now a rapid volley of rifle fire came from behind the Old Finch Place. Two shots followed this farther west, perhaps up near the firetower hill. Ray knew that with the breeze being southeast, at least a few of these deer would head upwind toward the big swamp. Chances are some of them will cross the Maple Grove Road on his planned runway and eventually pass his blind. He was confident, the mark of a good hunter.

Several times Ray turned to investigate deer-like rustles only to find the squirrels were now up and about. There were now black and gray squirrels in sight. Ray knew they were the same species and only different color phases. He remembered being a skeptic when the taxonomists came out with this information. Now if you search the wildlife archives you can find a picture of Ray's hands, holding a litter of little squirrels with both color phases being represented. Only then was he convinced that those college professors were right.

Ray enjoyed the antics of the squirrels, but didn't forget his objective for even a minute. Finally, the unmistakable sound of approaching deer came from the west. His fingers tightened on the rifle as a doe and two fawns passed his blind, only fifty yards to the southwest. He didn't raise the .243, as he had the deer identified the instant they appeared. The deer weren't in any hurry as they continued on toward the lowland brush south of Ray's blind. They entered the heavy cover, still within rifle range, about 150 yards away. Soon he heard a twig snap about where the other deer had appeared and Ray knew that it would likely be a buck following the three deer to the lowland cover. And it was the buck from the rye field. He raised the rifle as he pushed the safety off. When the four-pointer crossed a little opening, the rifle cracked and Ray and Archie had their winter meat supply supplemented with tender, good tasting venison.

"How many does that make?" Ray thought as he dressed out the fat buck.

He knew it was over fifty, as he had averaged a buck a year for as far back as he kept records. A buck a year for all of his deer hunting years, not a bad record for an old man. Some years no deer and the next fall a couple. It had been several years since he had failed to bag a deer.

"I hope they always keep the two-buck limit," Ray thought as he put the heart and liver on a sharp stick and headed off toward the house.

He left the dressed out deer next to his blind.

This time he took the direct route, straight north until he came out in the old field south of the house. It was grown up to brush now, but you could see the house soon after climbing through the remains of the of the old woven wire fence. As Ray started into the field, five deer came from the north and bounded past him only fifty yards or so from where he stood. The deer weren't aware that a hunter stood in the field as Ray had spotted them first and froze in his tracks.

"They sure are beautiful game animals," Ray thought as the deer left the field only a few yards from where he had been only a minute before.

Ray knew they had crossed the road just west of his house. He smiled to himself. The spruce trees are working.

Archie saw Ray coming across the field and put the coffeepot back on the stove. Ray went directly to Archie's house after dropping the heart and liver on his side porch.

"Well, how big was he?" Archie asked as he opened the door.

"One to eat, Arch," Ray replied, "but I do need a little help."

"Right after we have another cup of coffee, Ray," Archie said.

The men went into the kitchen and Archie poured, both black. The cups were quickly drained and the men went out into the garage and cranked up the four-wheeler. Both got on the machine and they went out into the road and turned west. Ray watched for fresh deer tracks and sure enough there they were, right where he had thought they should be. He pointed them out to his friend. They continued up the road and turned into the field after passing the little swale on the south side of the road. Ray didn't like these ORVs, and certainly didn't want to develop a trail into the field. Later he asked Archie to avoid running in the same tracks when they returned with the deer.

Ray and Archie had shared the cost of the four-wheeler when they realized that they couldn't get around the lakes in the winter, and it would be especially useful for pulling fish shanties. And, of course, deer out of the woods. The trip back to the rye field took only a few minutes.

"Let's stop here and drag the buck out here from the blind," Ray shouted over the roar of the little machine.

Less than an hour later the deer hung in Ray's garage.

"Venison liver for supper tomorrow night," Ray told his old friend.

The rest of the deer season was uneventful. Ray spent quite a lot of time in his blind, under authority of his second buck license. That was a nice legal offering, provided by the Michigan Legislature, several years ago. It allows successful hunters to continue enjoying their sport after filling their first license. Only does and fawns passed Ray's blind after his first day success.

"After all these years, I still enjoy watching deer," Ray thought as a doe and two fawns carefully picked their way past his stand.

Always alert, watching here and there, with their noses searching for that little drift of human scent that will send them off in a panic. They use their ears, rotating them back and forth like a radar antenna, listening for any stray sounds that might come from an enemy. If alerted to danger, they learned years earlier not to run too far or they run the chance of running past another hunter. Old Ray remembered when deer didn't behave with so much caution.

On his first unofficial deer hunt (he was too young to have a license), he jumped a single deer in the cedars on the west side of Deadman Lake. It was a perfect morning with a good tracking snow. The deer, that Ray naturally thought was a buck, ran a mile west almost to Snot Lake before breaking stride and turning off to the southwest toward Grass Lake. Ray never saw the deer and had to leave the trail as the evening shadows started to fall on the young hunter, now a long ways from home. It was well after dark when the young hunter reached home.

CHAPTER NINE

ONE FROSTY MORNING, RIGHT AFTER THE DEER SEASON, Archie awoke to the sound of a chain saw running back beyond Ray's house. He walked back to check on what was going on. Ray was falling all the big trees in the east/west fencerow that ran along the south side of the old field, about a quarter of a mile south of the house.

"This is the start of my wildlife plan, Arch," he said as his old friend approached.

"Didn't you ever learn to leave those dangerous toys alone unless you have someone along to pick up the pieces after you cut yourself?" Archie asked with a huff in his voice.

Ray stopped the saw and laid it on the tree stump left from the tree he had just fallen. He knew that Archie rarely raised his voice, and fully understood what he was just told.

"Yes, and at my age, I'm clearly in the wrong," Ray replied.

From that day on the chain saw never left the garage unless both men were together.

The tree-lopping project, as Ray called it, went pretty well.

He enjoyed Archie's company and they could take frequent breaks to discuss all kinds of things that helped to make their life together easier. Ray's plan was to create a dense tangle all around all the fields on the old farm. He knew that birds attracted to the down tree tops would bring seeds that would sprout and grow grape vines, briers, and all kinds of valuable plants that would grow up in or near the fencerow. He had seen it work on the game areas in southern Michigan, over fifty years earlier.

Now he wanted the lopped-tree fencerow to extend from Archie's line fence west to the rye field. Then it would turn south and go along the rye field to the southeast corner, before turning west and running clear to the old wagon trail, now only a foot path, that ran southerly back to the railroad grade. A crystal clear stream crossed the grade at that point and continued on to Deadman Lake.

A small brushy area protruded into the field just west of the little trail, so the project had to fall the trees along the two-acre margin. Ray was surprised that the trees here were as large as they were. He remembered the little woodlot as being filled with brush, sumac, and briers. And, of course, cottontail rabbits and ruffed grouse. Now the large trees would contribute to the edge effect that Ray wanted. After going around the two acre piece, the brushy edge would continue to the southwest corner of the old farm field before turning north and hence out to the Maple Grove Road.

Archie viewed the whole project as sort of a disaster affecting some perfectly good trees, now growing in the fencerow, but knew they were working on something that would produce game they both desired.

"This seems like a lot more shintangle than what's needed," he told his friend.

"Yes, when we're finished, I figure it will be over a mile. But we won't waste the trees we cut as we can chop them up for firewood when they dry out and by then they will have established some excellent fence-row cover."

Both men knew that they didn't have many years to enjoy the fruits of their labor, so they continued working on the project when the urge struck them, which was about three days a week. After all, they had to leave time for rabbit hunting which now had their highest priority.

"December is always the best month," Ray told his friend.

The work went well and before the nasty January weather set in they had about one half mile finished.

"It's better if we spread this out over a couple years, anyway," Ray said. "Next fall we can cut up some of the oak and maple for firewood."

Archie thought about that difficult job. Even without all the briers and grapevines that were sure to grow in the treetops, not all the trees fell exactly as planned. Most were perpendicular to the old fence, but some that had a mind of their own, fell lengthwise over top of those on the ground. They weren't going to be easy to extricate from the mess. As they reached the places where good deer runways ran toward Ray's blind, Archie suggested that they leave holes for the deer to pass through.

"We could even put up deer crossing signs," he jokingly said.

"Actually," Ray replied, "Deer won't wade through a lot of tree tops. I've seen it in the swamps when we used to have emergency browse cuttings to try to save starving deer."

But both men knew that there were natural openings along

the fence and deer would have little trouble getting through. If deer access to Ray's blind were a problem, there would even be a bulldozer working on the problem. Archie knew that Ray would let nothing stand in the way of insuring reasonable success during the last two weeks of November.

This December turned out to have a lot of days designed for rabbit hunting, and the old men made that their number one priority. The more they hunted the better Rex got. Ray quit going in to the swamp to help search out the rabbits. Rex did his own searching. His master now knew that he was 100 per cent deer-proof and that is a very satisfying feeling when you turn a hound loose in a swamp filled with wintering deer.

"Let's hunt the big swamp tomorrow," Ray suggested one day as they were winding down a morning of tree lopping.

"OK, breakfast at my place at 7:30 and we can get in the swamp before 9:00," Archie replied.

"I'll bring the lunches," Ray added.

That remark made both men think about their hunts when they were young boys, but neither said anything. Then, they hunted all day long without stopping for lunch. They might be miles from home and wouldn't waste time going back just to get something to eat. If they were lucky they might pick a few apples off the scattered apple trees found throughout their hunting area. But that would be all they had to eat. Neither complained. Now they needed their meals on a much better schedule. Their health depended on it.

Early the next morning the men headed back across Archie's "eighty" on the four-wheeler. Rex trotted along behind. This would be his first hare hunt in the big swamp and both men knew what was in store for the young dog. Today he would become acquainted with a real swamp and some long-legged hares. If Rex could have known, his head would have swelled with pride. The men had decided he had their complete trust.

They parked on the knoll overlooking the railroad grade. After loading their guns, they walked east on the grade until they reached the pipeline crossing that led southerly into the big swamp.

"Do you think the old pipeline still runs through the swamp on top of the ground?" Archie asked.

"I'd bet on it, Arch," Ray replied, knowing the difficult job of removing it or even trying to bury it. "I wouldn't be surprised if it isn't still being used."

As the men headed south on the pipeline right-of-way they noted a weathered sign, "Total Pipeline Company." And a short distance from the grade they entered the big swamp. The site was dominated by lowland brush, not white cedar as they had expected. Ray let Rex enter the dense cover on the west side of the trail through the swamp and the hunt was on. He knew the young dog would keep checking back, unless he hit a fresh hare trail.

"Dogs should hunt with you, not you hunt for the dogs," he told Archie. "When they get one up and running I don't hold them to that rule."

About a quarter of a mile farther south they hit the cedars and sure enough there on top of the ground ran the old pipeline, just as they had remembered. You could hear the thump, thump, thump of the oil being forced through the pipeline, clear from the Freeman-Redding field.

"They put a bigger pipeline through the swamp, just west of Farwell, in the late sixties. It ran through my brother-in-law's property before crossing the tracks and entering the swamp. Don thought they planned to clear a much wider right-of-way than necessary and he did his best to stop the project. All Don and my sister got out of it was a small payment for the land involved," Ray told Archie.

"They couldn't get away with that today because of the environmental protection laws," Archie added.

About then they hit the first snowshoe hare tracks crossing back and forth across the pipeline. A minute later Rex opened up on a fresh hare track. He was only a hundred yards or so west of where the men stood.

"Maybe we should just spread out and wait here," Ray suggested.

He headed south a couple hundred yards until he crossed a heavily used hare runway across the pipeline. That's where he waited. He could see quite a ways west into the conifers because of heavily browsed cedars that opened up the stand.

"Just right for the little .22 semi-automatic Remington Model 241," he thought.

He inherited the rifle from his brother, Elmer, when he died several years earlier. He had replaced the open sights with a Weaver K 2.5 when he realized he had to learn to shoot scope sights for deer. His old friend, Lyle, drilled and tapped the rifle in preparation for mounting the scope. Ray never practiced enough with scope-sighted rifles, so he learned to shoot them by shooting at deer. Right now, as he waited, he wished he had his old Model 74 Winchester .22 that he had given to his oldest son so he could train his sons how to shoot a rifle. Ray thought about the stories Archie told about all the rabbits "shot through the head" with the little Winchester.

"I'll bet I could still see the front bead if I had it with me today," he thought. "These trifocals are bound to help."

It was a quiet morning in the big swamp and Rex's clear chop voice rang through the morning air. But in spite of the stillness, Rex's hound music soon faded to the southwest. Ray knew that the way that young hound drove rabbits he and his old friend wouldn't have long to wait before the hare would turn back. Sure enough, after about fifteen minutes of standing in the still swamp the unmistakably sound of the chase returning reached the old men's ears.

Ray glanced south at the sound of brush breaking and saw five deer clear the pipeline in an unhurried gait, just to get out of the way of the hound and hare that would surely follow. Ray didn't worry, he knew that a hare was ahead of the dog. He smiled as the chase came back on a pace that just seemed to flow through the swamp. Unless you have owned a good hound you will never understand the feeling. But now Ray knew he had selected the right spot, as Rex headed straight at him. Suddenly, the chase turned sharply toward the south and Ray turned to see a large white hare clear the pipeline in one big bound. He took a couple shots at it before it disappeared in the cedars to the east. He knew he had missed. Rex came right behind, bellowing for the entire world to hear, and he never missed a bark. Ray and Archie loved it.

Now both turned their attention to the east side of the pipeline. This time the hare only made a small circle before heading back, right where Archie waited with his shotgun. Ray saw his old friend raise his gun and at the shot the hare crumpled in the snow on the pipeline right-of-way. Ray was pleased.

"Archie shoots Lew's Sweet 16 a lot better than he shot the old double," he thought.

"Hey, I saw another rabbit over there in the swamp, just before this one tried to cross," Archie hollered as his friend approached.

Rex must have known it, too. He barely muffed the dead hare before continuing across the pipeline to the west. In less than two minutes he opened up with another chase.

The second hare headed north until he hit the northerly edge of the heavy cover. Then turning west he went almost to Deadman Lake before heading south along the east side of the lake. Although Rex was almost out of hearing, his clear chop voice floated back to the men on a slight westerly breeze. Both knew exactly where the chase proceeded. Now as the hound and the hare reached the southeast corner of the lake they came to one of Archie and Ray's secret landmarks in the big swamp, a small ridge covered by aspen and a few white birch trees. When the hare turned east away from the lake, both men knew he was skirting the north edge of the little high ground in the swamp. Their memories of other hounds and other hare hunts occupied their minds as they waited.

Rex was close behind as the chase headed back toward the hunters.

"I've got to tell Archie a deer hunting story where the scene was that little aspen ridge," Ray thought.

But for now, he just stood still and listened to his little hound clearly telling his master to "watch out, he's coming back." Up to now there had been no breaks in the chase. Like Ray always said, a fast hound leaves a rabbit little time to mess up his trail. But now, running at full speed, the hare suddenly made a big jump of about six feet off to the side before continuing on toward the waiting hunters. Rex soon reached the break in the trail and immediately fell silent. Ray knew the problem and

smiled as he realized the young dog was doing exactly what a
finished hound should do. Rex returned to the spot where he
last had the trail and stopped to sniff this way and that until he
figured out what the hare had done. As he soon had the trail
straightened out, he opened up again in full cry. The mark of a
real hound!

"That hare has been chased before," Ray thought.

This time it had gained several hundred yards on Rex, but
the men knew that he was now close enough to them that they
better be alert. It was obvious; he would cross the pipeline near
where they waited. It wasn't a pell mell chase, as the dog was
still trying to get a good straight line to follow. The hare had
time to stop every few hops and Ray knew his chances with the
little .22 were greatly improved. Sure enough, the hare came
back and this time stopped in clear sight, about twenty yards
west. The .22 barked once and the chase was over. Rex continued to follow the trail until he came to the dead hare, lying in
the snow. He muffed his prey before looking up at Ray. His tail
was beating a happy rhythm, as only beagle tails can do. "Good
job, boss," he seemed to say. The feeling was mutual.

Ray picked up the dead hare, noticing that the little bullet
had hit it right behind the shoulder, not through the head.
Archie would notice. He did, but said nothing. "What say we
call it a day," Ray suggested. "Two good chases and two rabbits
in the bag. Not a bad day for a young dog and two old men."
With that, Ray put the leash on Rex and the threesome headed
back to the four-wheeler and home. They even enjoyed eating
their lunch in Ray's kitchen. Sandwiches washed down with a
fresh pot of coffee. Ray had let Rex come into the house and he
found his usual spot in front of the fireplace, curled up on his

own rug. The promised dog pen never got built. Rex stayed in the house most of the time.

As the men sat at the kitchen table, Ray said, "I don't think I ever told you my deer hunting story about the buck and that little ridge on the southeast corner of Deadman Lake. It was 1958, I think."

"Here comes another story about the one that got away," Archie thought. Ray rarely talked about the others.

"Anyway," Ray continued, "You've heard me tell you about my old deer hunting friend, Lyle, who hunted with me for several years. Well, the deer season had been slow so Lyle and I decided to check things out back in Deadman Swamp. We drove out to the Wilds' place and stopped at the house. You remember Mrs. Wilds always let us go back to the lake on that two-track trail that ran through their yard, the one we used today with the four-wheeler. It was well past lunchtime, so we didn't have a lot of time to hunt or to visit.

"After she granted permission, we drove back to the knoll that we parked on today. After getting out of the car and loading our rifles we took our old footpath to the lake. Lyle decided to stay in that little opening just south of the place where we kept that old scow we used for fishing the lake. There was no snow on the ground, but we noticed a couple fresh buck rubs and quite a lot of sign. I thought his decision was a pretty good one. I left Lyle and continued south along the west side of the lake. I crossed that little feeder stream that comes from the west and flows into the lake and continued around the lake until I came to the outlet on the south side. If you remember, beaver usually kept a dam across the outlet a couple hundred yards south of the lake. That year was no exception, so I had to carefully pick my way across the dam to keep my feet dry. And, as you know, I was headed for our little aspen ridge southeast of the lake."

"I don't know the outcome of this story, but if you got a buck back there it would take a week to pack it out. That is unless you got him out with a boat," Archie commented.

"Yes, I thought about that, but I was in an exploring mood so continued my difficult hike," Ray continued.

"When I got across the dam and into that dense stand of cedars, I was really encouraged by the amount of deer sign in the swamp at that point. I continued northeast until I came out of the swamp on the knoll. Fresh deer trails crossed the little ridge and I expected a big buck to appear at any minute. Well, I found just the right spot and climbed up on an old white pine stump where I could cover most of the opening. You know the place with lowland conifers south, east, and north of me. Looking west, I could see the tag alders and marsh grass on the edge of the lake."

"Yes, I remember the spot, but we rarely walked around the east side of the lake because the going was just too tough. Even for young boys," Archie commented, "I guess the only time we did was when we were after ducks."

Ray continued, "Today when Rex took that snowshoe along the east side of Deadman until they reached our little island, I thought about telling you this story.

"Anyway, it was now late in the afternoon and the shadows were starting to fall. I knew it would be way past dark when I got back to the car, but Lyle had hunted with me for years and he simply would wait until I made it out of the swamp. My biggest concern was how to get the buck out of there, as you accurately assessed. And I certainly was about to shoot one, or so I thought.

"As I stood there on my stump, I glanced off to the north and there, just within the swamp margin, I saw an antler sticking up. The deer was obviously still in his bed under a big balsam and as it was late in the day I knew it would only be a few minutes before he would stand up to give me a clear shot. I congratulated myself for reaching this spot without spooking the animal. But you know how it is when it starts to get dark; you can imagine all kinds of things. Stumps become deer and so forth, but I had no doubt about it. There was a nice buck within easy rifle range and we were just trying to see who would make the first move. I couldn't see any of the deer's body or even its head. Nothing to shoot at, so I had to wait.

"Both his antlers were in plain sight, but darkness was fast setting in. I was carrying my .30-30 Winchester and had a great deal of confidence that I could flatten him if he gave me half a chance. Finally, in desperation, I decided to rush him and take my chances. If he ran straight away, which was most likely, he would be mine. I jumped down off the stump and closed the distance to the buck in record time. There he laid in his bed, deader that a mackerel. He was curled up in the most natural position, I believe it would have fooled anyone. He had been shot behind the shoulder and it was obvious to me that some hunter had simply failed to follow the nice buck into the swamp."

"Well, you didn't have to drag him out," Archie added.

"No, but to this day, I've never forgotten my feelings at that moment," Ray said as he concluded his story.

Little did the old men know that only four years from now,

this forest opening in the big swamp would play a most important role in their lives.

As the winter wore on the men continued to work on the wildlife habitat project. At winter's end they had a little less than half of the tree lopping finished. The cottontail rabbits were having a great time chewing on the tender branches provided by the fallen trees. Occasionally a ruffed grouse would flush from beneath the treetops when the work crew arrived for their customary half-day work. The men knew they could rout out the rabbits if they tried, but for now they decided to save them for seed. When they went hunting, which was often, they hunted hares and more than half the time in the big swamp. They never took more than two rabbits a day.

"We'll just take what we need to eat, and an occasional one for Mrs. Thrush," they decided.

On some days Rex drove the hares way off to the southwest, clear out of hearing. After waiting for a long time the hunters would head off across the swamp to their secret island in the swamp. There they could almost always pick up the voice of the little hound, still on the trail. Often they would move in and pick up the dog without bagging a single hare on that day. It really didn't matter to the old men. It was the excitement of the chase that was the main reason they were in the swamp, just like the old days.

One morning after finishing their second cup of coffee in Archie's kitchen, Ray brought up the topic of fishing.

"Next winter we should get my pike-spearing shanty out and supplement our rabbit diet with a few northerns," he said.

"Good idea, Ray," Archie said. "Do you think we could put it out on Cranberry Lake?"

"I doubt it, Arch," Ray replied. "We should have speared up there when Lew was the caretaker for the property."

Both thought about the days when they had access to the big private lake. The duck hunting was fabulous and the fishing was out of this world. Neither took advantage of the situation, as they didn't want to put Lew's job in jeopardy. They wouldn't hunt on the property because most local folks called it a game refuge. But they did very well on ducks on the beaver ponds just west of the lake. Lew would transport them across the lake well before daylight and come to retrieve them later in the day. Ray was quiet for several minutes and Archie wondered what he was thinking, but said nothing.

Ray was thinking about the early days on the old farm. His dad and Mr. Finch would hook the horses to the sleighs, load up their spearing shanties and go up to Cranberry Lake to spear pike. It would be well after dark when they returned with the wagon box on the sleighs covered with huge northern pike. They would leave their shanties on the lake for a couple weeks and would fish two or three days a week. None of the fish went to waste because all farm families considered them part of Nature's bounty, to be shared with everyone in the neighborhood.

"Those were wonderful days," Ray thought, but he was really too young to remember much about them. That was even before Archie lived in the area.

Ray finally broke the silence, "Arch, do you remember when we borrowed Mr. Finch's fish shanty and put it out on Grass Lake?"

"Yes, if I remember correctly it was a two part shanty, so it could be handled easier," Archie replied.

Both men thought about that expedition; it really was quite an operation for two young boys.

"I remember how excited old Lew Finch was when he helped us get everything ready," Ray added. " First we had to get the shanty in shape and then find all the fishing gear that Mr. Finch had stored away for years."

After everything was ready, the old man told Ray that he could borrow his beloved old horse, Jim. On the day selected for the two-mile trip, the boys loaded the fish shanty on a stone boat because no sleighs were left around the farm, and the would-be pike spearers set off for the little lake southwest of the farm. A bog surrounded the lake and they couldn't get old Jim clear out to the lake because they didn't want to take a chance with him falling through the floating carpet.

"Remember what a terrible time we had wrestling that shanty out on the ice?" Archie asked.

"Yes, and then after we cut the hole with double-bitted axes and then watched down the hole all day without seeing even a minnow swim by, we went through the whole operation again. I'll bet we were never so tired in our lives" Ray replied. "Arch, did I ever tell you my dad's favorite story?"

Archie listened as his friend continued. "Well, late one afternoon Pa and his buddy returned from ice fishing on Littlefield Lake. After waiting until after supper because he thought his dad might be in a better mood then, he asked my grandpa, 'Pa, is something lost when you know where it is?' 'No, I guess not,' Grandpa replied. This gave Pa his opening; 'Well then your new double-bitted ax ain't lost because it's on the bottom of Littlefield Lake.'"

"I think we ought to put the shanty out on Five Lakes," Ray

suggested. "I speared there quite a lot when I was in high school, but now I hear they put a dam in and the lakes are all connected. There used to be some big pike there and we ought to be able to get a few."

"Well, I don't know. I never got into the spearing like you did," Archie said.

Ray remembered. Archie's parents had died and he moved to Colorado to live with his brother Lew. Ray also understood that Archie had married young, but they never discussed their first marriages. Both ended in divorce and those things are sometimes better left buried in the past. Both old men knew why they were ignoring the ice fishing during this their first winter back home. They were just too busy, with a new dog to train and all the habitat work to do. Next winter will be different. Rex will forgive them if they take a little time off to fish.

Even during the next summer the old men didn't fish much. They caught a few bass out of Deadman Lake and fished for bluegills three times, once each in Clear, Bear, and Gray Lakes. Ray kept busy implementing his wildlife habitat plan. He hired the same young farmer that had put in his rye field to plow up the field that laid southwest of where the barn had stood on the old homestead.

After the ground had been worked up, Ray planted corn in the five-acre field. The young farmer laughed at the way he went about it. The field was checkrowed and planted with an old hand planter that Ray had found at an antique store. Again, the young man thought that Ray "had lost his marbles" when he showed up one day with an old cultivator and asked that the field be cultivated three times during the growing season with this old implement.

"I'll keep the thistles under control with a hoe," Ray told him.

Ray even had to show him how the old cultivator worked. They had to borrow a team of horses to pull it. Fortunately, a mutual friend owned horses that were used in horse-pulling contests at county fairs.

Ray knew what he was doing, although many around him thought otherwise.

"Clean farming hastened the end of the excellent small game hunting we enjoyed," he told Archie.

And hoe thistles he did. This time he wore shoes in the thistle patches.

"I'll bet the world would be a better place if all kids had to hoe thistles on hot July days while barefooted," he told his old friend.

Ray's cornfield even impressed his farmer friend. Rainfall was adequate and hot August days really made the corn grow. Of course, he didn't tell everyone that he had used one of the new hybrid varieties. He hadn't completely lost his mind.

Quite the contrary, old Ray had something else in mind when he planted the cornfield. Was it strictly a field providing extra food for stressed wildlife? No. But you would never get the old man to discuss it, not even to his friend Archie.

In late summer Archie noticed that Ray would often take hikes to the west side of the old farm. He never asked his friend to accompany him, which Archie thought strange, but didn't feel the need to press for an answer. Usually these private walks took place in late afternoon and as that was a time for both men to be thinking about what to cook for supper, enough occupied their mind without getting into what was behind Ray's strange behavior. To thoroughly understand what took place you would have to get into Ray's mind and, of course, no one was permitted there. Not even the old man himself.

After reaching the old homestead, Ray would proceed to the spot behind where the old barn was once located. Then, finding the remains of the old lane, turning west from the barn lot, he would go west up along the north side of the maturing cornfield. Then, he would be overcome with emotions and seem to be a small boy accompanying his dad on an evening walk, "to watch the corn grow" as his dad told him almost seventy years earlier. His little hand would be tightly held in the big rough hand of his father as they proceeded up the lane about half way to the woods to the west. Then they would turn into the tall corn and his father would explain how the rain and hot August nights helped to produce the crops that they and their livestock needed.

No, Ray wasn't losing his mind. He was just reliving those precious moments that were so rudely taken away from him when his father had the heart attack that made him physically unable to take any more of these little hikes with his son. His dad lived another six or seven years, but something was missing. Ray couldn't remember his father being anything but a physically handicapped person. He was a wonderful man, taken from his young son right when the little boy needed him most. Now when Ray walked into the corn, he would stop to offer a prayer to God. Then, with tears in his eyes, he would turn and retrace his steps back to his new home. Often, he would go to bed without supper.

When fall came the corn was left standing in the field. About the middle of October the old men would start taking their guns afield. Archie carried the 16 gauge and Ray the little .22. Rex would chase the cottontails between Archie's swales and the lopped fencerows on the back of Ray's place.

"Lots more rabbits around this fall," Archie remarked one day as they stood behind Ray's house listening to the beagle drive a rabbit.

Both men knew that the habitat plan was paying dividends. Even though the small game season had been open for two weeks the old friends had waited for colder weather before starting the fall harvest of rabbits and other small game.

Ray said, "It's nuts to hunt when the only decent thing to do is go fishing."

Even after starting the fall harvest, they only shot a few rabbits for food. "Don't think we need to can any, do we Arch?" Ray commented.

One morning as they left Ray's house for a little hunt, Archie noticed that Ray carrying his shotgun, a Model 11A, Remington autoloading shotgun.

"Where's Rex?" Archie asked when it was obvious that the little beagle had been left in the house.

"Well, today we are going to do things a little differently. I didn't tell you because I thought you might back out," Ray told his old friend.

Archie knew, but said nothing. Today they were going to try for partridge. With that, the men loaded their shotguns and crossed the field to the east end of the lopped fencerow. Wild grape, briars, and other grouse foods had already started to form a tangle in the treetops. And, of course, the tender tree sprouts made the old fencerow especially attractive to grouse and rabbits. The old men had flushed some pats during their rabbit hunts, but Ray had held his fire, waiting for this very moment.

When they reached their objective, the east end of the lopped treetops, Ray asked, "Want the inside or the outside, Arch?"

"You better take the inside, Ray," Archie replied.

Ray knew that his old friend was still worried about how he would do on flying targets, and most birds would fly toward the heavier cover to the south.

"OK, but next time you're on the inside," Ray agreed.

The men hadn't gone fifty yards up the fencerow before a grouse rocketed up out of fallen treetop and headed off toward the lowland brush to the south. Ray's shotgun boomed and the bird tumbled to the ground, a few feathers floating behind.

Archie saw the grouse fall and hollered, "Good shot, Ray."

Ray put the bird into the game pouch on the back of his old hunting coat and the men continued west along the fencerow. Right in the corner, where the cover turned toward the south, three birds took flight. Two went over Ray's head and headed off toward his deer blind. He tried for the second one and missed him cleanly. The third bird flew out of the cover right at Archie and then cut east directly away from the hunter.

The 16 gauge roared and Archie shouted, "I got him. Did you get yours?"

"No. There were two of them and they are still going," Ray answered.

They soon completed their hunt along the part of the lopped tree fencerow that had been completed. Ray bagged one more grouse out of two more flushed.

"Not bad, Arch, three birds in the bag out of six flushes," Ray said.

"I guess you knew what you were doing when you started this project," Archie commented.

Ray smiled but said nothing. The two ruffed grouse in his coat felt pretty good.

When the men reached Ray's house, he said, "If you want to leave your pat, I'll clean them and then we can have a big feed tomorrow."

"OK, if you promise to make that partridge casserole," Archie replied.

So the deal was made. Here's the recipe:

PARTRIDGE CASSEROLE
Ingredients:
Two or three ruffed grouse (skinned and cleaned)
2 cups of white flour   1/2 teaspoon of salt
1/2 teaspoon of pepper   1/4 teaspoon of paprika
2 eggs   1/2 cup of milk
1 can of cream mushroom soup
1 soup can of water

Directions:
Cut grouse up into 2-3" chunks. Mix dry ingredients together. Beat eggs and milk together with a blender. Dip pieces of meat together in eggs and milk batter. Brown ruffed grouse chunks in hot skillet greased with olive oil. Place in casserole and add soup until meat is well covered. Bake in oven at 325 degrees for 1 hour. Enjoy!

Right after dinner the next night, the men retreated to Ray's living room. The fall air had a chill in it, so Ray had built a fire in the fireplace earlier in the day. Now it glowed through the doors of his fireplace insert and made it toasty warm in the room.

"Maybe not quite as nice as an open fireplace, but you don't lose all the heat up the chimney either," Ray commented.

"Yes, I'd like to have one in my fireplace. But I just don't have enough wood on my place to feed an insert all winter," Archie replied.

Ray thought about it for a moment before saying, "That's no problem, Arch. We'll just cut wood on shares, out of the lopped trees. I think you already cut more than your share, when we cut up some of those maple and oaks last week."

"That would be fine with me, Ray, but what will we do when we use up all that wood supply?" Archie asked.

"Well, as they say, we'll cross that bridge when we come to it," Ray answered.

So early next spring Archie put in his fireplace insert. Just like Ray's and just like the one in Ray's Pentwater house. Both men figured that model was the best on the market.

With their discussion of the warmth of the fireplace completed, Ray remarked, "You know I can't believe it. It's only a couple weeks before the deer season. What say we take the pickup and your portable spotlight and go back and shine the rye field?"

"That seems like a good idea to me. You get the truck out and I'll go get the light," Archie said.

A few minutes later the men were driving down the road past the little swale and turned into the field and headed off toward the rye field. Archie had plugged the spotlight into the cigarette lighter socket and immediately started to shine the field looking for deer.

"I noticed you got a pretty good catch of rye again, in spite of it being drier than last year," Archie commented.

"Yes, but we have to be careful not to open the road up back there, or we will have all the deer shiners in the county checking up on our deer. And unfortunately, some of them will be packing their .30-30s," Ray replied as the truck approached the green rye field. "It's the peak of the rut, Arch, and unless I miss my guess we are about to see something exciting," he added.

Ray had already noticed the Big One's tracks crossing the road west of the house, so he was convinced the big buck was still around. Also, at the conclusion of the grouse hunt he had checked the rye field and believed the same deer had been there, too. Now as they approached the rye field, Archie cast the beam across the green field. Deer eyes were shining all over the seven-acre field. Several deer were quite close to where Ray stopped the pickup. They were all does and fawns. Suddenly, the old men saw a huge buck enter the woods near the southeast corner of the rye. Both men were convinced that he was the Big One.

"He sure looks like a ten-pointer this year," Ray excitedly said.

"Boy, did you see the spread to those antlers? That's the biggest buck I ever saw," Archie added.

Ray thought about other big bucks that had crossed his path, but said nothing. He didn't want to take anything away from Archie's excitement. After all, what will it take to get him to join in on the hunt on November 15?

"I never tire of watching deer and when you see one like that it gets the old adrenaline flowing," Ray said.

With all the deer out of the field, Ray turned the truck around and headed back to the house. That night he laid awake and thought about the big deer. He judged that the buck was now three-and-a-half years old. Ray couldn't know that he and Archie had another two years to watch the Big One as both old men now called the big deer. By now, Ray knew that he wanted to bag another big buck and set plans in motion that he hoped would eventually lead to success. He thought his worthy quarry was about the same size as the two largest ones he had managed to bag in sixty years of hunting.

"Probably near 200 pounds, dressed out," Ray thought.

A few days later, Archie heard rifle fire out behind Ray's house. He knew Ray was out there checking the sight alignment on his deer rifles. He hesitated to walk over, as he knew the pressure he would face. But he loved to see Ray shoot, and a few minutes later he stood behind his friend.

Archie watched as Ray put bullet after bullet into the black of the target about a hundred yards away. The bullets were being fired from the .243.

"Scopes and mounts are a lot better today than when they first came out. I rarely have any adjustments to make," Ray said.

"This sure is a sweet shooting little rifle, Arch. How would you like to try it out?" Ray asked.

He got Archie's standard reply, "No thanks, not today."

Ray had a feeling that his friend was weakening. Perhaps there was some significance in the "not today."

He quickly added, "That big buck has to leave the rye field either to the south or to the east, past my blind. We can go back there about 200 yards south of the field and build you a blind. That way we can pretty well cover his route to Deadman Swamp and we just might get him."

Ray had no way of knowing, but if they had done that the year before it would have worked out. This year was different. The big buck had learned from his last year's mistake. He would be in the swamp before the first streaks of light lit up the morning on opening day. And, Ray was comfortably nestled down in his blind, waiting patiently. Archie was snug in his bed, just thinking about getting up and preparing breakfast.

It was a cold, clear morning and the glow of Ray's lantern warmed up the inside of the blind. This heat source was now a necessity. His doctor had warned him about staying out in the cold weather. The young MD knew he would be ignored.

"This old man will likely die with his boots on," he thought.

Ray's sons thought the same thing. But they knew what the deer season meant to the old man. You might say they even encouraged him to continue hunting.

They heard him say, over a hundred times, "I want to die at ninety-nine years old, dragging out a ten-point buck I just shot."

Of course, some men wanted to live just as long and then be shot by a jealous husband. It's just a question of priorities.

With the first light of dawn, shots started to ring out. Some were a long way off, but some were close enough to give Ray the special excitement of the first morning. He thought about some of the bucks he had bagged over the years. A high percentage of them had been shot the first day, usually before 10 am. He wondered why other hunters always got the first shooting. He thought about one buck that offered him the first chance. It slipped past his stand so early that he couldn't quite make out the antlers, so he let it go even though he could clearly see the swollen neck of a buck in the rut. Shooting mistakes just weren't permitted in Ray's camp.

Shortly after daylight two ruffed grouse thundered up out of the cedars south of the blind and landed on the slight slope that led up to the blind from the swamp. They were only about fifty feet from the old man hidden in his blind. They craned their necks this way and that to insure their security. After walking a few feet in the crisp leaves they started to utter that chirping noise that Ray knew signified immediate flight. Sure enough, off they flew toward the lopped fencerow, north of the blind. They almost took Ray's hat off when they cleared the hunter's head by only a few feet. Their flush can scare a young hunter out of two years growth, especially when it's unexpected. A few minutes later Ray's "pet" squirrels came out and started to chase each other around.

"They sure spend a lot of time playing around before getting down to the job of feeding," Ray thought.

All the leaves were down and the ground was frozen, so any movement made by these creatures of the forest could be heard at quite a distance. Even old Ray's ears could hear the squirrels, now over a hundred yards from the blind. Ray already knew that any deer that might have been feeding in the rye field had left the field in a southerly direction at daylight.

"That's right where Archie should have been waiting," he thought. "Oh well, they will just be bigger next year."

Then Ray heard a rifle shot drift down from the north on the slight northerly breeze. He knew it came from across the Maple Grove Road, and was probably just on the north side of big leatherleaf bog on the old Finch place. Almost immediately three more shots rang out in quick succession.

"Sounds like a miss to me," he thought. "Come on, spruce trees do your work."

Obviously, he hoped the deer would come south and cross the road west of his house. It was now almost ten o'clock and Ray hadn't seen a single deer. He never lost his enthusiasm. That's one reason he was such a good hunter.

"If you expect defeat, that's what you will get," he always told his sons.

It was almost eleven o'clock when Ray heard the unmistakable sound of a deer approaching from the north. "No there are more than one," he thought. His hopes shrunk a little. Sure enough, a doe and two fawns trotted past the blind about sixty yards to the east. Ray watched them as they picked their way through the few cedar trees on the edge of the swamp and entered the lowland brush. Suddenly, he was aware that another deer was following the first three. He knew from experience that is the one to check out. He shifted his weight on the milk carton to get a better look.

He saw a single deer disappear behind a witchhazel clump about seventy yards to the southeast. The deer stopped, just out of sight. It didn't move for a good five minutes and Ray thought it had given him the slip. He could feel his old heart thumping in his chest from the excitement of the moment. It didn't worry him, as he never had the old deer hunter's bugaboo, "buck fever." He thought of his old deer-hunting friend, Richard, that he had hunted with for over twenty-five seasons. Dick was a good rifle shot, but at times like this he had trouble. He bagged a lot of deer, but he missed many, too. And he and Ray had to track down several after they got past his stand.

Ray didn't have to worry. The deer was still there. Suddenly he came in plain sight with a bound toward the cover of the swamp. He didn't run fast, like a spooked deer, but just made it for the swamp on an easy lope. Ray was on him instantly as he saw antlers when the buck cleared the witchhazel clump. He followed the deer in his scope until he had him lined up just right and then pulled the trigger. The little rifle barked as only a .243 does. The buck stumbled slightly, but entered the thick cover "full speed ahead." No chance for another shot, but Ray knew another was not necessary. He clearly heard the deer breaking a lot of brush as it headed off toward the south. And then nothing but silence. Ray just sat tight. A bluejay broke the stillness with his scolding from the swamp edge. Ray knew he had meat in camp before he left the blind about ten minutes later.

"Could wait a little longer if I was worried about my hold," Ray thought. "I'd guess that one is about a six-pointer."

He entered the swamp, exactly where the buck had disappeared and quickly found the blood trail. About sixty-five yards farther the six-point buck lay dead on a little hummock in the swamp. Ray took off his coat and hung it on a broken branch. Then he took out his sharp hunting knife and carefully dressed out his trophy. He didn't hurry.

"Take time now and you won't be sorry later when you start eating the venison," he taught his sons.

He noted that the little .243 bullet had hit the deer right behind the front shoulder, passed clear through the chest cavity. A lung shot. That was his favorite hold on a deer, as any deer hit there won't go very far.

When the work was done, he turned the animal over on his belly to drain. Then he got the tag from his coat pocket and tied it securely to an antler. After putting on his coat and picking up his rifle he headed back toward the blind. He left the buck lying in the swamp, as he needed Archie's help in dragging him out. Besides, he didn't worry about other hunters stealing his winter meat supply. He had walked away from many and never lost a single one.

He smiled when he thought about one that he had taken the time to hide. He shot that one in a hay field, and as it lay right in the open, he dragged it over to a tag alder swale only a few yards away. Then he covered it up with marsh grass before heading off to find his friend Lyle to obtain help getting the deer out to the truck, parked over a half mile away. When he and Lyle returned it took them over an hour to find the buck. And that was only a small swale right in the middle of a big alfalfa field.

When Ray reached his blind he blew out the lantern and carried it with him as he headed back to the house. This time he walked back to the rye field and took the easy route back. He cut straight out to the Maple Grove Road and then walked down the road to his home. He really wanted to check to see where the deer crossed the road on the way to his blind. Sure enough, there were the tracks right on his prepared runway. As soon as Ray reached the house he entered the garage and put the heart and liver in a bucket of cold water to soak. He always dumped in a generous supply of salt to help get rid of any surplus blood.

"That helps to improve the flavor of the first venison of the season," he told his old friend, Archie.

Rex greeted his master at the door.

"What are you up to, leaving me home while you go off to the woods with a gun?" he seemed to say.

Then he got a strong whiff of deer scent off Ray's clothes and knew he had no business being along on this hunt. He didn't want anything to do with those trash game animals.

Ray then phoned his old friend. " We got one to drag out," he said, "Not a big one, but not one to look down your nose at either. A nice six-pointer."

"Great," Archie said. "I'll be right over with the four-wheeler."

When Archie drove up a few minutes later, Ray sat at the kitchen table eating his lunch that he brought back from the blind. After pouring his friend a cup of warmed up coffee, the men sat at the table while Ray told his story about bagging the buck. That is part of the deer hunting tradition.

Two hours later, the deer was hanging in the garage. Both men showed the strain of the effort and needed to sit down to rest for awhile.

"You know, Arch, we can't drag deer out of the woods for many more years. The four-wheeler helps, but I just about gave out while we were getting that buck up out of the swamp," Ray said.

Both old men were thinking the same thing.

"I never heard of anyone hiring young guys to haul out their deer," Archie replied.

Both men had grown sons, but said nothing about bringing them in on the hunt. Archie's boys didn't hunt and Ray's lived too far away. Besides they always hunted together or with their buddies. As soon as the old men got their second wind, the subject was dropped and would not come up again until the next time they had a deer to drag out.

The rest of the deer season went by without anything too exciting to report. Again Ray, armed with a second buck license, spent several days in the blind watching squirrels, partridge, and a few does and fawns pass by. He never got bored with the situation, even though he saw no more bucks. He loved the woods, the clear fresh air, and the sounds you never hear unless you are there. He knew he was there as a predator and at times like these he seemed to share his thoughts with his primitive ancestors. He was always aware that over the years and especially at the very moment of success, with a nice buck dead at his feet, he would be overcome with a warm glow that seemed to say, "We won't starve again this winter." He was convinced that was the exact feeling that primitive man had at times like these.

CHAPTER TEN

ONE NIGHT IN EARLY JANUARY, RAY PICKED UP THE TELE-phone and called one of his old rabbit hunting friends, Pete Petoskey. After exchanging pleasantries, he got down to the business at hand.

"Got any good rabbit dogs, Pete?"

"Sure, I've always got one or two around that will chase rabbits or hares, but right now the snow is so deep that their bellies are dragging. We're just waiting for the stuff to settle down before getting out again," Pete replied.

As Petoskey lived at Lewiston, Ray knew what was meant.

"Well, that's why I called," Ray said. "We've only got about six inches of snow on the ground and we've been giving the hares fits."

"You mean you finally got another beagle?" Pete asked.

"Yes, that's why I called. I knew you had a lot of snow, so I thought I might be able to talk you into coming down here for a couple days of hunting," Ray replied. "My new dog is less than two years old and running pretty well, but he needs to run with other hounds. I bought him from a field trial guy, so I know he was trained with other dogs." Ray answered.

Pete understood why Ray wanted to give his new dog some experience running with other hounds. A dog that is so independent that he won't "hark in" to other hounds will spoil the chase for hunters who enjoy putting down two or more beagles at a time. You can't blame the dog. You must blame the hound owner for failing to provide young dogs the competition they need in their first two years. Both Ray and Pete enjoyed pack chases and spent a lot of time together running some pretty good hounds in their younger days.

So arrangements were made and a few days later Pete rolled into Ray's yard. It was late afternoon on a Sunday. They avoided the weekend, so it was likely that they would have the swamps to themselves. Ray invited Archie over to meet his old colleague and friend and to have supper together. Ray had one of his favorite meals simmering on the stove, a big pot of venison burgundy. Now all he had to do was cook the noodles to go with it. Pete hauled his stuff into Ray's spare bedroom and made himself right at home, as Ray knew he would.

"There never was anyone exactly like Petoskey," Ray had earlier told Archie. But that's another story.

Now here is the venison burgundy recipe:

VENISON BURGUNDY

Ingredients:

Two pounds venison round steak	Three slices bacon
One small can mushrooms	One cup Burgundy wine
Two beef bouillon cubes, crushed	1/2 cup flour
1 teaspoon salt	A couple pinches of garlic powder

1/4 teaspoon each of pepper, thyme, marjoram.
1/2 teaspoon seasoned salt

Directions:

Fry the bacon in a large frying pan until crisp. Break up the bacon into small pieces. Cut the venison into small cubes and shake them in a paper bag with the flour until the cubes are well coated. Add the bacon bits and the cubes to the frying pan and brown the cubes thoroughly. Drain surplus fat from the pan. Next add all the dry seasonings and the wine and bring the whole dish to near boiling. Don't boil! Now put the venison and all, in a Crock-Pot and cook on low for 6 to 8 hours. The meat should be extra tender. Add the mushrooms and turn the heat to high for another 1/2 hour. This dish is delicious when served over noodles.

After supper the men went out in the yard to get acquainted with Pete's little hounds. Rex was allowed to follow. After all, they would be his companions for the next couple days, too. Pete had brought two beagles and they were busy checking out things from a nice dog box in the back of Pete's station wagon. Ray judged the beagles to be about three years old. Perhaps the oldest would be four. He was right. He also knew they would be deer proof or they wouldn't be living in Petoskey's kennel. Archie excused himself and went home. He knew he would be part of the next day's hunt.

"Breakfast at my house at 7am, Arch," Ray told his friend.

As Archie left for home, Pete opened the station wagon back door and freed the two beagles from the dog box. Keeping the dogs close at foot, Pete and Ray carried the dog box into the garage. Then Pete got out dog dishes and dog food and fed the little hounds. When they had finished eating the men took them outside and waited for them to do their jobs. Then Pete called them in and put them in the dog box for the night.

"Pretty fancy quarters," Ray remarked. "I remember when our hounds had to sleep in the car trunk."

"Yes, I believe we both have more money now then when we were working. Even our dogs live better," Pete replied.

"Those are good looking hounds," Ray added. "If they run as well as they look, we're in for some exciting hare chases during the next couple days."

Both dogs were females and Ray guessed they would both measure over thirteen inches. Rex was a little bigger, so Ray knew he would have no difficulty keeping up with the chase. With everything in order, Ray and Pete went in the house and had a little nightcap before retiring for the night.

The morning came early and Archie arrived in time to help get breakfast. The three men gathered around the kitchen table for a big breakfast of pancakes and eggs, promptly at the scheduled hour - 7 am.

"This is the kind of breakfast we need before heading off into the swamp," Pete remarked.

Archie had made sandwiches and brought along a big thermos bottle filled with black coffee, so the men were prepared for a long day in the swamp.

About an inch of snow had fallen during the night, but the air was still. The temperature was just a few degrees below freezing.

"This is going to be a perfect day for rabbit hunting," Ray said as the men went outdoors and prepared to load up for the trip to the swamp.

He really wanted to get Pete into the big swamp, but decided to put that off until the next day. That would give the hounds a day to get acquainted and run a few hares where Ray could keep track of how things were going.

"I think we ought to start out in that swamp up in Garfield Township where we used to hunt, Pete," Ray suggested.

"You're the guide," Pete responded.

After loading the dog box with the two beagles still inside, the men got in Pete's station wagon. Archie rode in the front seat and Ray piled in the back, with Rex snuggled up close beside him. He had to hold him down because he was busy checking up on his new friends who were prancing around in the dog box behind him. It only took fifteen minutes to reach the cedar swamp selected for the day's hunt.

The hounds hadn't been in the swamp five minutes when Pete's oldest dog opened up. The other female harked in and away they went toward the east. Ray didn't wait for Rex to join in. He took off through the cedars, calling his dog and urging him to join in on the chase. Rex ran over to check up on all the excitement and when he got a whiff of hare scent took off after the older hounds. It didn't take him long to catch up and soon the men knew that all three dogs were running together. Rex hadn't forgotten his early rabbit chasing days when the professional handler that planned to make him into a field trial dog started him. He knew how to run with other hounds.

"Now Pete's two beagles will get their legs stretched, " Ray thought.

All three old hunters knew when Rex took the lead. You could tell the cry of the smaller beagles that now found them running as hard as they could to keep up. But, keep up they did and soon all three were running as one hound. The old saying was, "you could cover them with a blanket." About then the hare made a sharp turn in an effort to shake the dogs. All three fell silent when they reached the check. It was only a couple of minutes before Pete's old experienced hound figured out the check and the chase was on again.

Ray returned to the edge of the swamp and found Archie

guarding an old tote road near where the hare was started. As Archie hadn't hunted this swamp before, Ray took a minute to explain the lay of the land to his old friend. He drew a rough sketch of the swamp in the snow.

"This old tote road goes northeast to near the middle of the swamp and then swings toward the east. I'm sure it's so grown up now that you couldn't follow it clear through the swamp. Right where the trail peters out you will find Petoskey, as that is his favorite stand when the dogs are running. You can hear them from there no matter where they go. If you run a compass line straight east from that point, you will come to a black spruce swamp that has a leatherleaf bog along the east margin. Then you break out of the swamp to an oak and pine ridge that runs north and south along the east side of this swamp. I'm going back to the road and go north and then cut back to the east along the north side of the swamp."

With that, Ray headed out to the road and came out near the station wagon. He planned to go farther north before cutting back to the east, but by then you could clearly hear the hounds returning. As they were driving hard, he knew it was likely that the hare would come clear out to the road. He hurried up the road for a hundred yards or so before taking a stand, watching east and as far into the swamp as he could see. He knew he didn't have a good spot, but that didn't matter. He was being treated to some of the best hound music he had ever heard.

Ray smiled as he realized he had made the right plans for this day's hunt. The hounds stayed in hearing for the whole circle. Now all three hunters knew the hare was coming back, and being driven hard by a pack of beagles that ran like they had always been hunting together. And this was only their first hare, together as a pack! Ray thought that Archie was about to be run over by the white hare. He knew that the old experienced rabbit hunter would be waiting. Suddenly, his 16 gauge barked once and only a minute later the dogs fell silent.

Pete immediately started to call his hounds. "Heya! Heya! Heya! Here Lady, Here Lady, Heya! Heya! Heya!"

Ray knew Pete had seen another rabbit. When the dogs responded to his calls, he put them on the trail. Pete had jumped the hare when he first went out in the swamp, so it took the little beagles a while to work out the cold trail. They led off to the north with only an occasional bark to let the hunters know what was going on. Rex was with the older hounds, but remained silent. The dogs followed the trail for almost ten minutes before opening up. The hunters knew the hare was now up and running. If Ray had reached his original objective that hare would have come straight to him.

The dogs now drove the hare north, clear out of the cedars and into the lowland brush fringe on the north side of the swamp. Then they turned east and headed for the east side of the swamp and the black spruce thicket. Ray knew where he should be, so he went to the north side of the cedars and cut into the swamp through the lowland brush until he reached his goal, which was a red maple opening in the swamp where he had bagged many hares in past years. Sure enough, the dogs and hare had already been across the south edge of the little opening. Here he waited.

He had no trouble following the chase. The dogs went clear to the east side of the bog, before turning south.

"Wow! Listen to those hounds drive that hare. You'd think they always hunted together," Ray thought.

Petoskey was down in the middle of the swamp, on his favorite stand, smiling and thinking the same thing. Even Archie was pleased. He knew he was being treated to some super hound music and he really enjoyed it.

After circling the bog, the dogs turned back to the west and came straight at Pete. They were traveling like a horse race. Ray knew old Pete loved to hear such hound music. Shortly, Petoskey's .22 barked once and the dogs fell silent. Ray decided to head south through the swamp to where Pete was now letting the dogs muff the dead hare.

"You guys earned it," he told the little beagles.

Just as Ray entered the dense cover on the swamp edge, away went a big cottontail. It turned off to the east, full speed ahead. As he couldn't get a bead on the rabbit in the thick cover, he didn't shoot. Anyway, that's what beagles are for.

"Here Rex! Here Rex! Yuk! Yuk! Yuk!" he hollered at the top of his voice.

Rex heard Ray and took off to see what was up. Pete's dogs stayed behind with their master. Rex reached Ray in only a couple minutes.

"Right here, boy," Ray said as he pointed out the trail.

Rex knew there had to be a hot track here someplace and started to smell this way and that. When he hit the fresh trail, he let out a big yip. This was immediately followed by the steady chop, chop, chop, of a beagle in full cry. Every rabbit hunter likes to listen to his own dog on the trail of a cottontail or hare. And Ray was certainly proud of Rex. He not only was good, but he had a beautiful voice.

Rex was well to the east before Pete's dogs joined the chase. That was good sign that the beagles from Lewiston had already learned to trust the young hound. This time the dogs didn't just head off for the other end of the swamp. Being a cottontail, the quarry took time to dodge and circle in some of the toughest thickets in the swamp. Finally, when he failed to shake the persistent hounds, the rabbit left the swamp and cut over the oak and pine ridge to an old farm field. The field was now covered with upland brush, with a few scattered pines. The scattered openings were covered with dense grass and sweet fern. A perfect haven for cottontails.

Now the rabbit took full advantage of the different cover type and laid a most difficult trail for his pursuers. A slight breeze that scattered the scent in the more open situation added to the hounds' difficulty. Now Pete, too, knew the dogs were chasing a cottontail. Ray thought about going back to get Archie, but gave up on that idea when the chase went so far east. He left the swamp and took a stand right where the dogs followed the rabbit to high ground. Soon Ray heard the brush breaking behind him and turned to see Pete come out of the swamp.

"That a cottontail?" he hollered over to Ray.

"Yes, I saw him when I jumped him back there in the swamp," Ray replied. "The trail left the swamp right here. Let's spread out and see if we can bag him when he comes back."

Both men were armed with semi-automatic .22 rifles, so the outcome was far from certain. But who cares? They were there to listen to hound music.

The beagles had been silent for over five minutes, so the hunters were thinking that the rabbit had given them the slip. Or perhaps he had holed up. Suddenly came the "Yi, Yi Yi, Yi. Yi," of beagles on a sight chase. Both men knew the rabbit had waited out there in the field and then jumped up right in front of the dogs. They now knew he would be coming back to the swamp "like a scared rabbit" and their chance of hitting him would be pretty slim. Sure enough, he came to them under full power. The cottontail crossed only about fifteen yards north of Ray and in only a few more leaps he would be safely in the swamp. Ray's little .22 barked once, twice, three times. On the third shot the rabbit folded right in the middle of a big bound and skidded to a stop in the oak leaves and snow. The hounds were right behind, but overran the dead rabbit as they rushed past. When they lost the scent, they fell silent. Now Ray was most pleased when they turned as one and quickly found the dead rabbit. Ray let them maul it around for awhile before picking it up. The dogs were still trying to wrest the rabbit from Ray's grasp when Pete walked up.

"Where did you say you got that beagle?" he asked.

" I told you, I bought him from a beagler who planned to run him in field trials," Ray replied.

"Come on, old friend. We both know they don't sell any like that one," Pete stated.

"Well, Rex measures over fifteen inches and can't run the big trials anymore. Lucky for me, but too bad for the beagler," Ray explained. "I knew what I wanted, so went to a lot of field trials until I lucked out," he added.

"Let's head back toward Archie or he will get hungry and eat up all our lunches," Ray suggested.

So the hunters turned west, followed by the little hounds. They cut straight across the bog and soon entered the black spruce thicket. Hare trails were everywhere.

"Maybe we ought to put the dogs on leashes," Pete commented.

"No, let them search. If they get another one up we can let them run, while we eat lunch," Ray replied. "They are a lot younger than we are and it wouldn't hurt them to get the extra workout."

Sure enough, the men hadn't gone more than one hundred yards before all three beagles opened up on a fresh hare trail. This one went straight west, straight at Archie. Ray was hoping that his old friend would still be standing on that tote road in the swamp. He didn't have long to wonder, as Archie's shotgun soon boomed and the chase was over.

"Let's hurry out there and catch the dogs before they get another one up," Pete said.

So the old men picked up their pace and soon reached Archie and quickly got the little beagles on leashes. They continued on to the station wagon and Ray was pleased when he saw Pete open the dog box and put all three hounds in the box. The old men then sat in the car and enjoyed their lunch while they discussed the morning hunt. No one hurried to get back out into the swamp.

Finally, the conversation turned to deer, as it always did when Ray and Pete were together. Pete was very interested in Ray's habitat work and especially how successful it was turning out. He suggested they pass up the late afternoon hunt and visit Ray's old homestead. It was now almost 2:30pm and all three hunters thought that would be a good idea. So Pete cranked up the car and they headed back toward Ray's farm.

"Let's take Rock Road and then we will come in on the Maple Grove Road from the west," Ray said.

A few minutes later when they reached the old homestead site, Ray suggested they turn off the road right where the old family driveway used to be. Pete didn't want to get stuck in the loose snow, so he parked on the road shoulder. The men got out of the car and walked across the yard to where the old house had stood.

"You are now standing on the exact spot where I was born," Ray said.

Then he gestured toward the south to where the old barn had stood.

"I cleaned up the old homestead site and had everything bull-dozed into the basement hole of the old barn. Then when that was done, I seeded the whole area to our old clover and grass mixture that we used on the game areas over fifty years ago."

"You mean you still remembered what to plant?" Pete asked.

"No, I just called Marv Cooley and he sent me the seeding mixture," Ray replied.

Then the men walked out to check the cornfield.

"Pretty good corn for up in this country," Pete observed. "How come you didn't harvest it last fall?"

He knew the answer. A few minutes later, as they walked through the standing corn, it was obvious. The field was riddled with deer tracks. Fresh cottontail tracks were found along the old lane and they led out into the weedy cornfield. Even the squirrels were coming into the field from the woods to the west and dragging ears of corn back to the fencerow where they probably felt safer while feeding.

"This is the way a corn field should look, Ray," Pete remarked.

All three men laughed when Ray said that only gentlemen farmers could grow corn like this.

"My plan is to leave this field just as it is for two years. There ought to be enough corn to feed the critters for two winters," Ray told his friends.

As the day was getting late, they didn't spend much time looking at the lopped fencerow.

"Come back in about two years and I'll show you a real wildlife paradise," Ray said as the men walked back to the car.

They then drove back to Ray's house. After feeding the beagles all the men pitched in and cleaned the rabbits. When finished with the chores, Archie headed for home. Ray told him that they would pick him up at six o'clock and they would go out to dinner at the Doherty Hotel.

"Why don't I drive and that way I can be the designated driver?" Archie suggested.

All agreed that would be a good idea. With that Pete and Ray entered the house and after washing up, sat down in front of the fireplace with a drink to celebrate old times.

"Archie rarely drinks anything, so this is a good idea to have a couple here before leaving for supper," Ray told his old colleague.

"Yes, and drinking at home is a lot cheaper, too," Pete added.

About an hour later Archie picked them up.

As they headed down the road toward Clare, Ray said, "Tomorrow we hunt the big swamp."

The next morning at nine o'clock the men were on the back of Archie's "eighty" getting ready to enter the big swamp. Archie had made two trips from the house with the four-wheeler. On the first trip he hauled Pete with his two hounds trotting along side. Then next, he brought Ray and Rex. They left the ORV on the knoll north of the railroad grade, crossed over, and entered the cedar swamp.

"How come we never hunted here in the old days?" Pete asked Ray.

"I always figured we didn't have time, as this is a big swamp," Ray replied. "I'm sure you remember that even by sticking to smaller swamps, we were often busy rounding up hounds well after dark. Then we had to drive the hundred miles home to wives who sometimes didn't appreciate serving warmed up supper at ten o'clock."

Ray knew that Pete would understand what he meant.

Archie and Ray had decided to introduce Pete to the big swamp by first going in to Deadman Lake. They followed the footpath to the little lake. You could tell that Pete was quite impressed by the natural beauty of the unspoiled lake. The lake was frozen over, so the men crossed the ice to the aspen and birch ridge on the southeast side. Of course, Ray had to tell the story about the dead buck that laid under the balsam and fooled him so badly over forty years earlier. Pete enjoyed the story as he, too, had often hunted with old Lyle.

"Archie and I decided that we wanted to save our energy for more important things, so we didn't get here by crossing on the beaver dam down there on the outlet at the south end of the lake," Ray said as he pointed to the south.

Up to now the men hadn't crossed a single hare track, but had flushed a couple ruffed grouse soon after entering the cedars northwest of the lake. The lack of hare sign hadn't surprised Ray. First, he had to show Pete the little lake. Now when the hunters entered the conifers on the north side of the aspen ridge, hare tracks and trails were everywhere. Some hares had been out along the edge, chewing on aspen sprouts that had come in around an old windfall. Also, a lot of aspen regeneration grew along the lakeshore where beavers had cut part of their winter food supply. The hunters didn't have long to wait. The dogs hadn't gone far along the swamp edge before Pete's oldest hound let out a "yip." A bark or two followed this as the little beagles worked out last night's hare tracks. After about ten minutes of cold trailing, all three hounds opened up on a hot scent. The hunters now knew that a hare was up and running.

"What's the plan?" Pete asked.

"Let's just stand here and wait to see where the chase leads, before we decide where to take stands," Ray said.

Then he looked to Archie for a suggestion, as the dogs drove the hare way off to the east. Both men knew that "you can't get there from here," and Petoskey would now get his introduction to the big swamp. The chase went east for several minutes before turning toward the south. Ray hoped the beagles would turn back toward where the hunters waited, but they didn't. Soon the hound music faded to the south and the swamp was suddenly silent.

"Well," Ray began, "The swamp leads off to the south for about six miles. There is an east/west gravel road over there about three miles and it crosses the swamp. I'm sure the dogs will head back before crossing that road. If we went back to the beaver dam and crossed over to the west, we could find an old logging road that goes out to the high ground. Then we could follow the swamp margin to the southwest for a half-mile and perhaps get close enough to hear the dogs again. In my younger days I'd already be across the beaver dam, but now I think we should just spread out and wait here."

Pete looked shocked and looked at Ray, "I heard you talk about Deadman Swamp, but I didn't know it rivaled the Deadstream."

"That's only the half of it," Ray replied, "if you head east you can stay in swamp conifers all the way to Farwell and that's over two miles. However, man has left his mark and there are a couple pipelines running north and south through the swamp. The first one is over there about a half-mile and I hope we will end up there later today. That pipeline is pretty well grown up to brush, but Archie and I can find it without much trouble. Also, we know a few of the swamps secrets and can find a few openings and an aspen ridge or two. We spent a lot of time chasing hares and fishing brook trout here when we were kids."

With that introduction of the big swamp out of the way, the men separated to wait for the hare to return. All three hunters felt that uneasiness that all beagle owners must suffer when their dogs go out of hearing. A penalty you must pay if you want to chase hares. Archie went back to the outlet and took a stand in the open cedars near the beaver dam. There he could clearly hear the little stream gurgling as it flowed over the beaver dam. But the flowing water was not loud enough to keep him from hearing the dogs, when they returned. Ray walked over to the north edge of the ridge and entered the cedars until he reached the spot where the hare was first routed from his daytime bed. Pete went east along the ridge and took a stand right where the upland ended on the cedar margin. They waited.

Another twenty minutes passed before Archie, who had the best ears, heard the dogs returning from the south. The beagles were really driving and it was only a few minutes later when Ray heard Rex's clear chop. He knew that all three hounds were running together, but Rex's voice was just a little louder. Soon Pete, too, could hear the pack returning.

"They are driving that hare with all their might," Ray thought. "I sure hope we don't fail them now."

He felt more comfortable when he realized they were heading straight to the waiting hunters. When the chase reached the ridge, Pete's .22 cracked twice. But the chase continued west along the swamp margin right toward Ray. He soon saw the big hare, floating through the cedars like "a gray ghost." When he was only fifteen yards from the waiting hunter he made the fatal mistake of stopping to try to figure out how to get rid of those pesky beagles. It was an easy shot and this one was shot right through the head.

Ray carried the dead hare back to high ground. The dogs followed along, still worrying the animal.

"Boy that was quite a chase," Pete commented as they met. "I know it's early, but let's stop for lunch and give the dogs a break."

Archie soon returned from his stand and the old men built a fire from the remains of a white-pine stump. Perhaps the very one Ray had stood on when fooled by the dead buck. When the fire was going they fed it with some dead branches from an oak. No one wanted to toast sandwiches with a smoky pine fire. When they had a good bed of coals, they cut forked sticks from a red maple and sat on a log near the fire to toast their lunch.

"Everything tastes better toasted," Ray commented as he turned his sandwich on the forked stick.

The men didn't tie up the dogs, so they had to call them back to their campfire several times. They wanted to get back to hare chasing. After a cup of hot coffee the men were ready, too.

"Let's work around the east side of the lake out toward the grade," Ray suggested.

Archie didn't want to leave the warm fire. He had just started to tell Pete about the good old days when he and Ray had hunted the big swamp. The last hare, shot through the head, offered the opportunity for Archie to stretch the truth about Ray and his .22 rifle. Ray enjoyed the stories, but reminded his friend that his memory wasn't quite right.

"Don't forget, Arch, our thirteen inch hounds didn't drive the rabbits so fast and the shooting was easier."

All the men laughed, as they realized it's easy to forget the misses and with a .22 there are a lot of them. Besides, Pete had hunted enough with Ray to know that he knew how to shoot the little rifle.

"Sure wish you could have seen this swamp then, Pete. Cedar boughs clear down to the ground and lots of ground hemlock, too," Ray said. "We usually hunted the finger swamps north of the railroad tracks, because it was easier to keep track of the dogs. They seldom went out of hearing out there, nor did they ever cross the railroad tracks," he added.

With that the men left the fire and headed north along the east side of the lake, toward the railroad grade. The beagles were busy searching for another hare to run, but still followed the hunters through the heavy cover to the north edge of the swamp. They came out just east of the four-wheeler, so Archie crossed the grade and left the thermos and the lunch leftovers at the ORV. He didn't want to carry them down in the interior of the swamp and he knew that's where they were now headed.

The hunters proceeded east along the north edge of the swamp toward the first oil pipeline. They hadn't gone far before Rex stumbled over another hare and the chase was on. The other two dogs harked in and the old men stood and listened to the dogs drive the hare to the east. Archie decided to stay put, but Pete and Ray moved down the swamp edge to follow the dogs. The beagles were setting the swamp ringing with their bell-like chop voices.

"I love it," Pete said. "I'm glad I finally got a hearing aid that works."

After a short run to the east the chase turned toward the south and Ray thought the dogs would soon be out of hearing. But he was wrong. The hare only went a short way before turning back toward the hunters. He passed Ray and Pete, just out of sight in the swamp and continued west to where Archie waited. "Blam," went his 16-gauge and the chase was over. Soon Archie joined the other two hunters and they proceeded east toward the pipeline. The dogs had already disappeared in the swamp, as they wanted to get another chase going. It didn't take long. They soon opened up, directly south of where the men moved along the edge. They trailed slowly at first, as this was not a really fresh trail. Perhaps it was a hare that had moved to get out of the way of the dogs when they were on the last chase. This hare led off to the southeast for some distance before the dogs announced the trail had turned hot. Then the hounds turned south and in only a short time the men were aware of a slight breeze rustling the evergreens. They hadn't noticed it when they had hound music to listen to. Now the swamp was quiet. The dogs had gone out of hearing.

"Let's go over and spread out along the pipeline and we'll have a good chance to bag him when he comes back," Ray suggested.

When they reached their objective and turned toward the south, Ray noticed Pete looking at the browsed out cedars.

"It's hard for our old colleagues to realize that I remember when deer were practically absent here," Ray told Pete.

Now it was obvious that a lot of deer were wintering in the big swamp. Archie stopped on the first hare runway and Pete and Ray continued to the south. They soon came to a place where a lot of hares had crossed during the night.

"I think I'll stay here," Pete announced.

"Hey, Look!" Ray shouted as five or six deer bounded across the pipeline about 200 yards south of where the men stood.

They were heading west and the hunters thought they might come back when the beagles returned with the hare. They didn't.

"Probably slipped out to the south to high ground," Ray later thought.

But for now he continued on down the pipeline, searching for a better stand. About 150 yards south of Pete, he came to the south edge of a dense cedar stand. The cedars opened up so he could see 50 yards or so along the margin. Here he made his stand. He knew that it was likely that if the beagles were driving hard the hare would run the edge, right to where he waited.

Soon after settling down, he could hear the dogs way off to the southwest. Obviously, the hare had turned and now the chase led back to where the hunters waited. Ray glanced north toward Pete just as a large deer crossed the pipeline, going east. Ray instantly knew, The Big One! The big buck sneaked across with his head held low. He still carried his huge rack, at least ten points. The buck was about midway between him and Pete. Ray was pleased when he noticed that his old friend had seen the deer, too. He knew that a big discussion of the event would follow. For now, that would have to wait as all three hunters heard the beagles returning from the west.

"Those three dogs are equal to any pack I've ever hunted with," Ray thought.

He remembered old Queenie and wondered how she would do with these much faster hounds. It wouldn't be fair to put her down with these fifteen-inch beagles, because she would have a tough time keeping up with the chase. It would break her heart to have to run behind. Ray brushed the thoughts out of his mind. Besides, with Queenie the hares just didn't make such large circles.

Ray didn't know, but Archie was thinking the same thing. "I'll take the slower dogs," Archie thought. "Sure, in the old days Queenie and Spot often went out of hearing, but seldom clear over into Isabella County."

Ray had picked Rex because he enjoyed the excitement of a fast hound, so you pay the penalty of some long distance chases.

Now as the beagles returned you could almost feel the chase move. The swamp rang out with the excitement of the hounds. Each one telling the world, in their own way, "Here we come! Better watch out!" No one needed to warn these old experienced rabbit hunters. They were alert as the dog's voices drew near. Pete and Archie watched Ray, as they knew the hare was running the swamp margin, directly at him. Just then Ray saw the big hare bounding along through the swamp conifers and raised his rifle. It made a big sideways jump and then turned sharply off toward the north. Perhaps he had seen Ray raise his rifle, but it didn't matter. The opportunity was now gone.

"Now I can watch those dogs pick that check," he thought as he lowered his little .22.

The beagles came on and, as Ray had expected, over ran the trail. They were almost out to the pipeline, before turning as one, they returned to the spot where they lost the scent. Ray was pleased that all three remained silent as they worked out the check. All their tails were busy as they searched this way and that for the trail that suddenly had disappeared. Finally, again, Pete's oldest hound picked up the trail. "I got him, I got him," she seemed to tell the world. The other two wasted no time in getting on with the chase that led off to the north, toward Pete and Archie. About the time the dogs straightened out the trail, Pete saw the white rabbit coming through the cedars. The hare knew he had gained some on the dogs, so it just hopped a few times and then sat to check things out. Pete let the hare approach to within easy shooting distance and then shot him through the head. He told the other hunters that it was an easy shot. But Archie noticed, another head shot.

As the three hunters gathered on the pipeline, Pete suggested, "Let's put the dogs on leashes and call it a day."

"Good idea," Ray said. "A hare apiece and a lot of good hound music. That's what I call a perfect day."

As Ray and Pete snapped the leashes on the dog's collars, Ray noticed that Pete had one of those leashes with twin snaps on the end.

"The same as George Richey had when he came after Queenie and Bob, over sixty years ago," he thought.

As the men turned toward the railroad grade, Pete turned to Ray and asked, "Did you see that big buck?"

"Yes," Ray replied, "he's almost half again larger than any others in this neighborhood."

"I'm surprised that he is still carrying his antlers," Pete added.

"That's because he has been feeding in my corn field and as you know, well-fed deer keep their antlers longer," Ray said. "Archie and I knew that we had a super buck living in our neighborhood, but so far he has outfoxed the hunters. We even have him named. We call him The Big One."

"Well, that might be the largest buck I've ever seen," Pete commented.

Ray knew that was quite a statement. Petoskey had been around a long time.

CHAPTER ELEVEN

RAY AND ARCHIE DIDN'T HUNT RABBITS MUCH AFTER THEIR highly successful two-day hunt with Petoskey. Probably the main reason was that the weather turned bitterly cold, with a lot of strong northwest winds. The strong winds reminded Ray of how the wind would sweep across Lake Michigan and buffet his house on the south side of Pentwater Lake.

"We always pulled the boat by the first of October." he told Archie one morning as they sat at Ray's kitchen table enjoying their second cup of coffee. "Otherwise, the boat would take a real beating tied to the dock. And of course, I wanted to get all the fall chores done in preparation for the deer season."

Both old men knew that they could find some escape from the wind by hunting down in the interior of the big swamp. Yet, they had all kinds of excuses for sitting in front of their fireplaces and soaking up the special warmth given off by the wood fires.

"Hares taste too much like a popple after the middle of January," was Ray's pet excuse.

Archie wasn't fooled. They were just feeling their age.

One morning, bright and early, Archie showed up at Ray's house especially chipper.

"Do you remember the young guy who used to help Lew with the caretaker job up at Cranberry Lake?" he asked.

"Yes, I remember him, but I couldn't come up with a name or even a face after all these years," Ray replied.

"Well," Archie continued, "I ran into him in the bank yesterday and he invited us up for a little ice fishing."

"Does that mean pike spearing, too?" Ray asked.

"Sure, in fact he made it clear the invitation only included the spearing season," Archie replied.

That had always been one of Ray's favorite winter pastimes and being able to spear Cranberry Lake, as his dad and Mr. Finch did in the '20s, was an unfulfilled desire. The pike-spearing season had been open since January 1 and Ray's fish shanty sat unused in the backyard. It made a good storage place for outdoor tools and Ray thought it would never go on the ice again.

"That's sure good news, Arch, but we've got some work to do to get ready," Ray said.

Suddenly the day didn't seem so cold as the men made their way out to the fish shanty. It was well hidden behind the garage in the brush. They wrestled it out and over to the garage. Ray moved the pickup out to the driveway and the old men pushed the shanty into the garage, where they could work on getting it ready.

First, they removed the wood stove and replaced it with a small propane one that fit nicely in one corner. Then they filled in the twenty-four by twenty-four inch hole that was located near one end of the floor, and cut a square thirty-inch hole exactly in the center of the floor. Next they built two benches, one on each side of the hole. With these changes the hole was almost directly in front of the entrance door.

"Guess we'll have to put up a sign like Randy has over the door on his fish shanty, 'BEWARE HOLE IN FRONT OF DOOR'," Ray remarked.

Both men laughed, but they knew that falling through a spearing hole wouldn't be much fun. Neither had ever heard of a fisherman doing that, but both had known of ice fishermen falling through a hole in the ice that was not marked after someone moved their shanty. Ray always put brush in the hole when he moved his shanty or took it off the lake.

When they were ready, three weeks of the eight-week spearing season had already gone past.

"It's not too late, Arch, I can remember some winters when we didn't get our shanties out on Pentwater Lake until February," Ray commented. "Actually, we got very few zero days there. The big lake really affected our weather."

Now, with the excitement they shared when they hauled Lew Finch's shanty over to Grass Lake in the late '30s, they loaded the shanty in the back of Ray's pickup and hauled it the five miles to Cranberry Lake. After unloading, they returned and got the four-wheeler.

"George said we could keep it in that shed," Archie remarked as he pointed to an old boathouse on the shore of the lake.

There was almost a foot of snow on the ground and they had some difficulty getting out on the lake with the shanty and four-wheeler. Archie's friend George came out of the caretaker's house and helped them get underway. After fighting their way through the drifted snow on the shoreline, the going was easy and the ORV pulled the shanty with no difficulty. They headed straight north to where the lake narrowed. They stopped on the east side and augured a few holes in the ice, looking for about eight feet of water. After selecting the desired spot, they augured four holes, one for each corner of the hole in the shanty floor. Next, Ray got out his ice saw and sawed between the four holes. An ice spud and ice tongs made short work of the block of ice remaining in the water.

"This sure beats cutting the hole with a double-bitted ax, eh, Arch?" Ray remarked, referring to their experience on Grass Lake. "It even beats cutting the hole with a chain saw. Ice and water can sure screw up a good chain saw."

After clearing the snow back away from the hole the men slid the shanty over the hole. Then Ray entered the shanty and scooped the ice chips and snow from the hole. He used an old plastic colander like the one Jeanne had used to drain spaghetti. He smiled when he remembered her sputtering when her colander came up missing every winter. Finally, she bought Ray one of his own. The very one he now used. After placing short pieces of two by fours under each corner of the shanty, Archie got busy banking snow around the outside. The wood chunks would keep the shanty from freezing to the ice. When they had finished, they lit the little propane stove. Soon it was toasty warm inside. After getting warm, they went back outside on the ice and spudded a hole northwest of the shanty. Then they put a block of wood in the hole and ran strong quarter-inch rope to two eyelets imbedded in the shanty. When the "anchor" froze in, the men knew the shanty wouldn't blow away in a strong wind. Now they were ready for tomorrow's excitement, so they turned off the stove, got on the four-wheeler and returned to shore.

The next morning shortly after eight o'clock, the men drove up, got on the four-wheeler and sped off across the lake to their shanty. In a minnow bucket they carried a ten-inch sucker, their decoy.

"I still like a live decoy, Arch. The wood ones work pretty well, but the sucker will warn you when a pike is approaching," Ray told his friend.

Live decoys were new to Archie, so he watched with interest as Ray scooped ice out of the hole and rigged up the sucker.

"We need to put him down about four feet, but first untangle the cord on that spear and get ready," Ray said as he remembered one day when he failed to have the spear ready.

A big pike had rushed in and mangled his decoy while he worked furiously trying to get the spear ready. He was too late and the big fish got away! Now, the men had decided to take turns spearing.

"We aren't going to try to clean out the lake. Two fish apiece will be plenty," Archie told his friend.

Both men knew that the legal limit was five pike each, but four would be all they needed and even leave some for their neighbor.

"A lot of people worry about the spearers getting too many fish, including some fisheries biologists, but such thinking is a waste of time. Only once did I get five pike in one day," Ray said. "I have to admit that we do get some big fish though. I guess that's what makes hook and line fishermen so concerned. Then the lucky guy has to go and get his picture in the paper."

When Archie had the spear ready, Ray let the decoy down

into the hole. It was tethered on a short piece of monofilament, which was tied to a half-pound lead weight that Ray had carved to resemble a small fish.

"That way we have two decoys working for us," he remarked.

The "lead fish" was tied to a stout piece of fish line with one end running through an eyelet in the top of the shanty, so positioned so that the decoy rig hung straight down in the center of the hole. The sucker swam around and around in the crystal clear water and never got out of sight as the men waited. It wasn't long before a school of minnows swam past, just under the ice. Visibility was excellent. The fish shanty had no windows and was even painted black inside to cut down on outside light. Everything was perfect for peering down into the frigid water.

About a quarter after nine the sucker went into frenzy, as Ray had told his friend would happen when a pike was near at hand. It darted here and there, trying to escape its archenemy. But it was held firmly in place by the heavy weight.

"Here comes one," Archie whispered.

The pike came in under the sucker and lay there, eyeing his breakfast, or so he thought.

"Now Arch!" Ray said.

Archie threw the spear at the pike, but missed him cleanly. A big swirl in the hole and the pike was gone. The fish had been a good one of about seven pounds.

"Better luck next time," Ray told his friend. "But don't throw the spear at the next one. Just line him up carefully and then give the spear a sharp push. It's easy to miss them, as they aren't exactly where they appear to be because of the effects of looking through the water. Only experience will improve your odds."

The spearers only waited another twenty minutes before another pike came along. Archie got him with no difficulty although he was hit quite a ways back, just in front of the tail.

"Try to hit them just behind the head, and you will have better success," Ray said.

Archie's pike weighed five pounds, an excellent eating size. Now it was Ray's turn. They didn't see another fish until they were eating their lunch.

Then Archie announced, "Watch out! Here comes a good one."

This one made a savage run at the decoy and almost had it before Ray pushed the spear in the water and hit the pike right behind the head. The big fish carried the spear and line it was tied to back under the ice. Ray waited a minute before carefully pulling him back through the hole and out on the ice to join Archie's fish. This one weighed nine pounds, a nice chunky fish.

The men finished their lunch and waited, staring down into the water until their old backs and necks ached. About three o'clock Archie got his second fish, a nice eight pounder.

"These are nice fish, Arch. What say we call it a day?" Ray suggested.

Archie agreed, so they packed up their things and headed back to the boathouse on their sturdy ORV. Before leaving the shanty Ray had removed the sucker from the rigging and put the lead weight and all into a drywall bucket, drilled full of quarter-inch holes. He then hung the bucket in the hole and let it down well under the ice on a stout cord.

"Our decoy will be right there tomorrow, waiting for us. If we guard him well, he will last as long as we want to fish this winter," he told Archie.

When they got back on shore, Archie stopped at the care-taker's house and gave him a pike. Even though George lived right there with all those nice fish waiting to be caught, he did little fishing. So the pike was much appreciated. Archie offered to fillet the fish, but George said, "No problem."

After getting home Ray cleaned the fish and Archie took a nice fillet down the road to Mrs. Thrush. Then Ray started sup-per, a meal of fresh northern pike.

"Once you learn how to handle those Y bones, there are few fish any better to eat," Ray told his friend as they both pitched in to get the meal on the table.

Ray poured a couple glasses of his favorite white wine. Soon they were sitting at Ray's dining room table, finishing up the last of the fried pike fillets. After eating and getting the dishes in the dishwasher, the men sat down in front of Ray's TV to watch the evening news. The weatherman predicted a warming trend for the next week.

This prompted Archie to remark, "Rex won't like if we fish every day, so if it warms up and these northwest winds go down we ought to work out a schedule. Mrs. Thrush told me she would take all the extra fish or rabbits we wanted to give her. She really liked that last cottontail we gave her."

"OK, I agree," Ray said. "Let's run the hares on the nice days and fish on the others. However, I think we should spread our extra game and fish around the neighborhood. I guess we are the only ones around here with fresh meat in camp."

"Yes, that's pretty good for a couple old —" Archie almost said that four letter word, but held up at the last second.

So the routine was established. On nice quiet days they hunt-ed and when the wind blew a little they fished. On real stormy days they just stayed home. Some days neither man left his own house. Ray read several books and Archie went back to writing poetry. A few days in mid February were quite warm with thawing temperatures. The old men tried for cottontails a couple times without success. The rabbits just wouldn't cooperate. Even those that were sitting out promptly beat it for holes when Rex jumped them. They could have continued on to the swamp for hares, as they don't hole up. But walking through slushy snow wasn't either man's idea of fun. They just turned and went back to sit in front of their fireplaces.

Meanwhile Archie continued turning out poems. Here is one to enjoy:

BEAGLE, BASSET, BLUETICK, AND WALKER HOUNDS OF THE TIMES

One was named Spot, the other one Queen,
They were sure friendly and noses keen.

Well, Ray really cherished his little beagle friend,
It was always ready to run rabbits to no end.

Arch and old Spot got along fine, too. And combine
When Ray or Arch shot it was either his or mine.

Whether the Schofield cedar thicket or old Deadman
Swamp, we hunted the woods wherever we tromped.

One day while hunting a little swale, two rabbits came
Out, Hell bent for a run. This is where Ray and Arch had
Their fun.

Ray said to Arch, "Why are you firing at my rabbit over here?"
Arch said, "I'm not, I got one of my own to cheer."

Old Friends and Old Dogs, memories will never end.
They will be lived over, time and time again.

Arch Rogers

Most of the snow was gone by mid-March, so the men went back to lopping trees in the fencerow on Ray's place. They finished the job in early April.

"Well, Arch, we now have over a mile of fencerow completed," Ray said. "But I've got some other things to do before my wildlife habitat plan is done."

Ray waited for the wildlife shrubs he had ordered from the U.S. Department of Agriculture. He told the Area Conservationist that he wanted 3,000 autumn olive and 2,000 multiflora rose.

The guy looked down his nose and advised Ray, "You know they spread all over the place."

"I hope they do, because my rabbits and grouse like them," Ray replied.

Ray smiled when he remembered how every habitat biologist had told southern Michigan farmers that multiflora rose wouldn't spread. It did. With the birds' help, these rose plants could be found wherever the seeds had been deposited in bird droppings.

"No one sued us, and by now no one remembers," Ray thought.

Autumn olive is even worse. On the better soils it really takes over. He knew the light soils on the old farm wouldn't grow a multiflora rose living fence, but he knew the plants would do what he desired.

The planting stock arrived on April 10 and Ray hired three strong farm boys to put them in on weekends from school. Earlier he had located an old grub hoe and two tree planting bars from his brother-in-law's barn. He carefully explained to the young men how he wanted the job done.

"I want a row of autumn olive put in about eight feet out in the field from the lopped fencerow," he said. "The rose plants are to be planted in little clumps on the woods side. I'll mark these areas out for you."

With those instructions, he took the grub hoe and a planting bar and showed the proper way to plant these woody shrubs.

"I'll be with you most of the time, so if you have any trouble just let me know," he said.

And so these wildlife food plants went in on schedule.

As the planting crew was working one day, a pickup truck pulled into the driveway at the old homestead. A stocky young man got out and walked back across the field to where Ray and the boys were working. Ray knew it was the heavy equipment operator he had called the day before. He walked back toward the road to meet the man. They met at the north edge of the big gully south of the cornfield. Ray thought of all the good times he spent here sliding down hill when he was a little boy. The "canyon" as he called the big gully. Somehow it didn't look nearly as foreboding as it did then. It took some nerve to jump on his Flexible Flyer and speed off down the hill.

"We met at the right spot to discuss my ideas for dredging a pond down there at the bottom," Ray told the contractor as he approached. "I've already bored a few holes and we can get water if we scoop off a couple feet of soil. There's a hardpan down about four feet, so it might not be a good idea to dredge through that or we might just drain the whole pond."

"Do you want me to use a dragline, or would a small dozer work best?" the man asked.

"You know the answer to that better than I would," Ray replied as the two men picked their way down the steep slope to the bottom. "I want the pond to run the full length of this lit-tle valley and to be as wide as possible," Ray instructed. "If you can, I want a few islands placed here and there in the water."

Both men knew that water would fill any hole as fast as it was dug.

"I think this is a job for my small dragline or backhoe, Ray," the equipment operator said. "It will cost a little more, but the quality of the job will be much better."

Ray knew it would cost a lot more, with the cost of getting down that steep slope and set up to work.

"He'll have a bulldozer down here before he's finished," Ray thought, but said nothing.

"I'll charge you on the basis of number of yards of dirt moved," the young man said.

"OK, I just want a quality job and I'm sure you will do one," Ray replied.

With that they shook hands on the deal they had just made and the contractor left.

Ray stood there and visualized his pond. He made plans to plant some wildlife shrubs around the pond margin.

"I think I will stick to native species that come in naturally on ponds like this, if you have time to wait," he thought.

He knew he didn't have any years to waste, so he would just tell his new work crew to dig up the woody species he wanted there and put them in as soon as the pond was dug. The entire project would cost a lot of money, but Ray really didn't care as long as he got the results he wanted.

Ray then walked to the west and up the slope and entered the woods on his west "forty". As he walked diagonally across the forty toward the northwest corner of his property, he recalled the dense second growth of aspen, red maple, black-berry briars, and here and there a white pine that grew there when he was a boy.

"This was the best place on the farm to find ruffed grouse and if you hit it just before dark you could often flush them by the dozens," he thought.

He remembered finding grouse nests along the edge of the swamp conifers to the south and one nest in the aspens that he and Archie had found one spring. The hen bird had nested along side an old white pine log left from the lumbering days. Now you couldn't even find a hummock left from those logs, and it is next to impossible to locate a white pine snag. Ray knew those days were gone forever. He knew why that forty was so productive of partridge, so he started to formulate a plan to restore at least some of its productivity. Here again, it wouldn't be easy.

Deer and natural woody-plant succession had destroyed the finger swamp of cedar, spruce, and balsam that ran along the old railroad tracks for over a half mile. Ray remembered bagging his first hare only a quarter mile south from where he now stood. He knew the ruffed grouse had hung out in that dense conifer cover during the day and then flew out just before dark to feed in the aspen and briers. His first partridge had fallen to his Pa's 12 gauge when he was only thirteen, right there on the swamp's margin. A big gun and a little boy. The gun was a dou-ble-barreled, hammer gun and was almost as long as the boy who carried it. He was moving west along the swamp margin when the big cock grouse flushed near his feet and flew straight away from the young hunter. Ray cocked the right hammer as he brought the gun up. The grouse fell about twenty yards away.

"Now I'm a real hunter," he proudly thought. "Now I've got to get one of those big bucks."

Two years later he shot his first buck. A nice eight-pointer. The deer was shot with his 16 gauge double, loaded with "punkin-ball" slugs.

Now as Ray studied what he should do with his west "forty" he felt a tinge of frustration. He knew he could do little with the deteriorated swamp conifers to the south. Also, he realized that heavy grazing by cattle several years ago had practically ruined the potential for restoring healthy aspen stands on his property. As the former aspen stands were cut and new sprouts attempted to regenerate the sites, new growth was promptly chewed off by too many cattle feeding on the site. Another example of man's ignorance of environmental consequences of unwise land use.

Now Ray noted that only a few big-toothed aspen were scattered around the open landscape. Perhaps not enough to insure enough suckers to populate the site if he now cut them. However, that appeared to be his only option. He noted a few old beech trees standing northwest of his cornfield on the woods margin. He remembered some were there when he was a little boy.

Leaving this area he proceeded off toward the west to where a little cedar clump had once grown in the aspen stand. It, too, had been grubbed into submission by the hordes of grazing cattle. Only three or four knurled old cedar trees remained. He thought about the grouse nest that he and Archie had found here. They visited the nest several times and were greeted by the hen pat playing the broken wing act to keep the boys from finding her nest. It did not escape their sharp eyes, but they hid that fact from the female grouse so she would not abandon the nest. It worked and all eleven eggs hatched successfully.

Then Ray thought about one mid-December day when he and an older brother cut through here on the way to the swamp to the south to run hares. It was long after the ruffed grouse season had ended, but Ray's brother watched intently as Queenie worked out the telltale trail a pat had left in the new fallen snow. Finally, with a roar the bird flushed and headed off toward the lowland conifers about 300 yards to the south. As the bird cleared the trees his brother's shotgun boomed and the partridge fell to the ground, a few feathers floating behind. To say Ray was shocked would be putting it mildly. His family was taught to "obey the laws of the land." None of them ever did such a thing!

Ray's brother walked over to the fallen bird and picked it up. He smoothed the feathers with one hand as he took it over to a big white pine stump. Carefully placing the bird on top of the stump, he covered it with leaves before shifting a layer of snow over the concealed bird. Then he walked over to his little brother.

"That one's for Pa," he explained, "you probably don't know that he is dying."

Ray did know as his mother had attempted to tell him only a week earlier. But at thirteen years old, it was easy for the young boy to deny. So, Ray didn't enjoy the rabbit hunt that followed. He just stood in a swamp clearing and listened to Queenie run the hares. His mind wasn't on the hunt. And he tried to push the idea of an illegally taken partridge from his thoughts. His brother didn't forget. The plump bird went in his hunting coat pocket on their return to the house. The next evening Ray's father enjoyed his last meal of partridge. And a little over a week later, just before Christmas, he died. He was only fifty-three years old.

Even now, over sixty years later, tears came to Ray's eyes. He turned and walked the mile home. It was late afternoon. He went to bed early, without eating supper.

The next morning Ray got up early and hungry. He fixed a breakfast of pancakes and eggs, washed down by lots of hot black coffee. If things went as planned he had a lot of work to do. He called Archie to determine if he was available to help out. He remembered what Archie had said about going out in the woods with the chain saw without him along. So a short time later they were loading chain saw, mixed gas and chain oil into the pickup. They drove up the road to the west until they reached the half way point on the west "forty".

"I want to see how much suckering we can get out of these old big-toothed aspen," Ray told his friend.

"They look pretty sick," Archie correctly observed.

"Well, it's worth a try. Otherwise we have a big planting job ahead of us. I want aspen to dominate this site like it did when we were boys and I haven't seen much wildlife value from the hybrid species," Ray said.

So the men went to work and by noon several of the old big-toothed aspen were on the ground.

"We'll just leave them there to rot," Ray told his steady helper.

The old men put in a little time every day, except Sundays. And three weeks later every aspen on the forty acres lay on the ground.

"Now, we will see what Mother Nature can do," Ray told his helper.

He knew it was likely that some trees would have to be planted, but for now he could forget any management until next winter. Then he ordered 1,000 white cedars and 5,000 jack pines. Ray knew jack pine was not part of the original forest on this site, but no way would he plant red pine. The old hatred for that species, which the foresters liked to plant, often showed through. The white cedars were to replant that little clump that used to grow near the southwest corner of the forty. He planned to plant the jack pine in small clumps along the Maple Grove Road.

One day as Ray and Archie were finishing up the cutting the trees, they left the chain saw along the east boundary of the forty next to the lopped fencerow and walked back to check the corn field. As it was late winter, Ray wanted to get a fix on how much corn remained in the field.

"There's enough corn here to feed the critters next winter, so we'll just let it grow up to weeds this summer," he told his friend.

They walked the length of the cornfield along the south side. Then turning north along the east side they found two heavily used deer runways entering the field.

"You know those deer have been coming up here from the big swamp all winter," Ray said.

It had been thawing for several days and the deer tracks stood out in the muddy ground.

"Yes, I think you're right," Archie replied. "Do you remember when the deer used to come up to our apple orchard all winter? And that was a half mile from the swamp," Archie asked.

Ray remembered. He used to enjoy Archie's stories about watching the deer on moonlit nights.

Now, both men saw the track at the same time. There it was,

as plain as day. The Big One had been in the field last night. He had been taking advantage of Ray's breadbasket, the cornfield.

"After eating like this all winter, he'll sure be a Boone and Crockett buck next fall," Ray remarked.

Both men knew he carried a near record set of antlers for their area last fall and Ray's prediction looked like a sure thing. And it was.

Summer came early. May was warm and wet. June was unusually hot. The old men spent a lot of time in late afternoons sitting on Archie's back deck. They almost made a ritual out of it. They would sit there in the sun and reminisce about the good old days. Both felt these were pretty good days, too. And they would often admit so. Along about five o'clock Archie would get out the gas grill and they would cook up steaks or hamburgers. Sometimes even hot dogs. Ray would go home and prepare a tossed salad.

"We need our green stuff, Arch," he would tell his friend.

Every evening, just before dark, they would see a mallard or two pitch into the pond behind the house. They knew that at least two duck broods were being raised there. They often heard the hen mallards quaking and clucking as they went about the business of raising their families.

"Lot's of ducks this year. Maybe we should harvest a few of them this fall," Ray said.

"Not with steel shot, Ray," Archie replied.

"Well, all the ponds are full of water and most have nesting pairs hanging around. I even see a couple drakes back there on my new pond and there is no cover there either," Ray commented, still trying to interest his old friend in a fall duck shoot.

Ray had seeded the entire area around the new pond and

with the abundant rains the clover and grass seed had come through nicely. But, again, all the old men did now was talk about duck hunting. They enjoyed it immensely when they were kids. Yet, now in their second childhood, so to speak, they would never again take a gun afield for waterfowl. Ray often wondered why. They both loved roast duck.

One afternoon, as the men sat in the late afternoon sun, Archie asked about Ray's rye field.

"Well, I had my young farmer friend plow down the rye for a green manure crop," Ray replied. "He is summer fallowing it now and I hope we can get alfalfa established there later on in the summer. I'm going to have a cover crop of oats planted, so I can have a good deer pasture there this fall."

Ray went on to explain how the cornfield looked, too. It had grown up to a dense stand of annual weeds, as expected.

"Perhaps we ought to go look at it tomorrow, Arch," Ray suggested.

So the next morning found the men walking through the cornfield. Or perhaps it should now be called a weed field.

"It's a good thing we don't have any active farmers as neighbors, or they surely would be complaining about all the weed seeds I'm growing," Ray stated.

Suddenly a brood of pheasants flushed from the field edge. It was a hen and six five-week-old chicks. They were the first pheasants the men had seen on the north side of the swamp since the early forties. Ray had shot his first ring-neck here in 1940. Right after the war he had bagged quite a few pheasants in Gilmore Township, south of the big swamp. Seeing pheasants again made Ray think about those hunts.

"I had an English Setter then, Arch," Ray said, "probably, the best pheasant dog I ever hunted with. She was good on grouse, too, but never completely stanch on point. I spoiled her by letting her flush pats from heavy cover while I waited on the edge. It improved my shooting percentage."

"Yes, I've heard you talk about that old dog before," Archie replied.

But Ray ignored his friend's remark, as he hadn't quite finished his story. "I specialized on hunting ruffed grouse and often had one or two of my sons along. When Susie came on point in some dense streamside cover, I'd get stationed and then yell, 'Get 'em.' Away she went and the pats would come thundering up, right out of the tag alders or gray dogwood. They usually offered pretty easy shooting and I'd get one or two on most flushes. My young sons thought that their old man was the best game shot in the world. I later taught them that it was only a question of getting ready for the expected flush. Before the old dog died, the two oldest boys were shooting ruffed grouse on the wing."

"You know what, Ray, I think I remember that setter. Wasn't she the one that we took duck hunting on the west side of Cranberry Lake? If I recall she was just a puppy then," Archie commented.

"I'd forgotten that, but you're right," Ray replied, "One day she even found a couple ducks we'd knocked down. She developed into an excellent retriever, even for ducks. That is until the water got freezing cold."

Ray smiled when he remembered a big mallard drake that fell just outside the shell ice on a beaver pond. He had to strip down to his shorts to get that duck. No kind of urging would convince the setter to swim out after that one.

Sure Ray had other breeds of dogs, but they always had to take a back seat to beagles. He always had one or two in his kennel when his sons were growing up.

"There is no better way to teach young hunters. Every kid should have the opportunity to shoot rabbits ahead of beagles," he always told his friends.

When the Conservation Department wanted to conduct youth hunts using pen-reared pheasants, Ray made several people angry by wanting to substitute wild rabbits, driven before well-trained beagles. He lost that one and the youth hunts went on.

Ray growled, "That pheasant is there only because you put it there just before the hunt. What a way to teach kids what hunting is all about!"

Reminiscing. "Why do we old men do so much of it?" Ray thought as he and Archie sat on Archie's back deck one evening.

They hadn't talked much this time. Just sat there watching the sun go down. Earlier, they had enjoyed half a chicken each, grilled on Archie's grill. Ray finally opened the conversation.

"I guess you know that I went to Mt. Pleasant to see my doctor today. Well, he gave me some bad news. They want to confirm it with additional tests, but it appears that I am a candidate for open-heart surgery."

"I knew it was near at hand, but you didn't want to talk about it, so I kept still," Archie said, "they have it down to a science now so that it is practically routine. I'm sure in your case it will go OK. You are still in pretty good shape."

"Well, here it is almost Labor Day, so I told the doctor that I'd have to think about it for a spell," Ray said.

Ray didn't fool Archie. That meant it would have to wait

until after deer season. Archie was right. But, starting that evening, Archie noticed that Ray cut down his activities and took it pretty easy.

"He wants to be sure he gets through the deer season," Archie thought.

He wanted to give his old friend some serious advice, but remained silent, as was his nature.

In October, after a few hard frosts and with the leaves starting to fall, Ray often let Rex out to run rabbits. He never left the house with a gun. Rex was in his prime and there were a lot of cottontails around, thanks to Ray's habitat projects. Sometimes, after Rex had run for an hour or two, Archie would pick up his shotgun and go out behind his house to where the beagle was running and bag a rabbit or two. After Archie had done this for two or three times, one day he was pleased when Ray's .22 barked. He walked over to his friend and was pleased that he had shot a plump cottontail.

During the next few weeks Ray often joined Archie, but never announced, "Let's go hunting tomorrow." Archie noticed that the old man hadn't lost his touch. When the little .22 cracked, a rabbit was usually in the bag. "That old man is still the best rifle shot I've ever known. And to think that he credits my dad for his ability with a rifle," Archie often thought. Ray also noted that Archie shot Lew's Sweet Sixteen with deadly accuracy.

"I must say something to him about it," Ray thought as Archie knocked down a pat that flushed from the edge of the duck pond behind their house.

The next evening after enjoying a meal of fried rabbit and partridge at Ray's house, the men retreated to the living room.

Ray had a small fire going in the fireplace and it was especially cozy and warm. As they sat by the fire Ray opened the conversation.

"Arch, I've been watching you shoot that shotgun for some time now. It's too bad you didn't have one like it when we were kids."

He carefully avoided saying that Archie should have owned that one, as both knew "that one" would always be Lew's.

"Anyway, you are a deadly shot now," Ray added, "I always told you that your shooting improved when your dad opened up the choke on that old double barrel. All it took was to develop a little confidence, and you certainly have it now!"

Archie thanked Ray for his kind statements, and then sat quiet for several minutes.

Archie finally broke the silence, "Speaking of my dad, I was thinking about him today when you shot that rabbit, going full bore with one shot from your little .22."

"Yes, Archie, he was responsible for me learning to shoot," Ray replied.

Both men knew the details as they had discussed them several times, but Archie wanted to go over it again, so they did.

It came about as a chance remark. One morning Archie's father was telling the boys about some guy he had known that shot at the gun shows.

"He was billed as the best rifle shot in the world," the old man said. "Well, he told me how he trained. He tied a knot in his mother's clothes line and every day he would take his little .22 back in the yard and blaze away until the line parted and any clothes on the line would fall to the ground."

Young Ray was impressed. He went home and set about to

become "the best shot in the world." His Mother's clothes lines were wire, so he had to develop different tactics. He started shooting at tin cans and then graduated to smaller targets, the bases of spent shotgun shells. But he maintained the idea; shoot some every day. It was fortunate that he and Archie lived in the country, because no one thought anything about farm boys shooting away to their heart's content. No one thought anything about gunfire in the neighborhood. Fortunately, .22 ammunition was cheap. Even Ray could afford all he needed to shoot every day. When he first told Archie how it all came to pass, Archie was very moved by the story. It certainly was no different now, and to make it especially heart warming, it was all true.

A few days later Ray called Archie and said, "I feel pretty good today, so let's run the lopped fencerow and harvest a few ruffed grouse."

Archie was ready in a minute and Ray met him in the yard with his 12 gauge crooked over his arm. The hunters walked to the south toward the duck pond and were soon at the east end of the improved fencerow. When they passed the pond a pair of mallards vaulted into the air from a small section of open water. Neither man raised their shotguns.

"Sure is strange," Archie remarked, "I remember when we would crawl a half mile for that kind of opportunity."

Ray, too, wondered why he didn't shoot. But both men dropped the subject.

"You take the inside today," Ray said as they reached their objective.

Archie knew why. Ray now trusted his shooting and the outside was much easier to walk. Archie cradled the Sweet 16 with a special fondness as the old men started toward the west along the now brushy fencerow. He knew most of the action would come his way. They had traveled only a half-mile before Ray called it quits. They had flushed four grouse and had killed two, one each. Neither man felt bad about ending their hunt. Both for different reasons.

"Let's do it again in a few days, Arch, I know I've got to walk a little every day to get ready for deer season," Ray remarked.

"No doubt about it," Archie replied.

So the old men ran the fencerow twice a week. They did much better if they waited until just before dark. The grouse didn't fail them. They were always there. And as twilight fell, they would often flush them far out in the open field under the scattered thornapples as they headed back across the field toward their houses. These were easy shots. The hunters always got two or three birds and one evening they shot four.

"That's pretty good partridge hunting," Ray told his old friend.

Both men knew the lopped fencerow made the difference.

Ray got much enjoyment out of his habitat improvement projects. He knew the west "forty" would start to produce in a few more years. The aspen he and Archie had fallen had sprouted profusely and had developed into little clones, here and there across the entire forty acres. He felt certain that ten years from now the students from Central Michigan University would come here to see what one man could do to improve wildlife habitat.

Ray had discussed his thoughts with his son Randy. "I want young students to come here to see what can be done. But don't give the property to the college. They will just close it to hunting and destroy the real meaning of habitat improvement."

He thought of a small piece of his old deer hunting area. The Littlefield family gave it to CMU and they wasted no time in declaring it off limits to hunting.

"I guess a lot of folks would rather see the deer starve," he said. "Why haven't we been able to do a better job in selling the role of hunting in modern wildlife management?"

The thought bothered him deeply, as he had no answer.

CHAPTER TWELVE

ABOUT A WEEK BEFORE DEER SEASON RAY PHONED HIS youngest son, Andy. He had spent the afternoon at his reloading bench. He knew that Andy's wife had bought him a .270 Winchester for his birthday, so he loaded up two boxes of ammunition for him. He also loaded a box of .243s for himself.

"I got those shells loaded up for you, so why don't you come down and get them?"

"Good," Andy replied. "I'll drive down right from work tomorrow night."

"Fine. I'll cook that ruffed grouse casserole and you can stay for supper," Ray told his youngest son. "Oh, by the way," Ray added, "as you won't be using the old .30-30 how about bringing it along? I'll tell you why when you get here."

So the next afternoon, just before dark, Andy arrived. He came to the house with the old Model 94 Winchester cradled in his arms. The old rifle opened a lot of memories for Ray as he took it in his hands and worked the action.

"Still a smooth action in spite of seeing a lot of use," Ray said.

He then retreated to his reloading room and soon returned with the .270 ammunition.

"Here, now you can practice up a little before deer season," he told Andy.

A few minutes later as father and son sat at the dining room table finishing up the last of the partridge casserole, Ray told Andy why he wanted the .30-30.

"I guess you know that Archie has started to hunt rabbits and pats with me," Ray said. "Well, I'm still trying to get him out deer hunting. So far all I get out of him is 'not now'. I've been thinking that if I can get him a rifle he can shoot, he might weaken."

"That shouldn't be a problem around this house," Andy replied.

"All my deer rifles are bolt actions with right hand bolts," Ray explained, "and Archie has the same problem with those that you have. He shoots off the left shoulder. That won't matter with the little Winchester, as you know."

So Andy left the .30-30 and went home right after supper.

Early the next morning Archie heard the old .30-30 going off out behind Ray's house. Naturally he had to investigate. He walked over and found that Ray had erected a target on the far hillside and it had a four-inch bullseye instead of the regular two-inch bull that Ray usually shot at. As the spotting scope was set up, Archie watched the action through the telescope. Some of the bullets hit in the black, but a few holes were punched in the paper just on the edge of the bullseye.

Finally, Ray said, "Good enough. Deer aren't hard to hit, anyway. And you can't expect this little .30-30 to shoot as accurately as the bolt actions."

"What's up, Ray? Are you planning to hunt with your old rifle this year?" Archie asked.

"Perhaps, but that's not the reason I asked Andy to bring it down to me," Ray answered. "Seeing you raised the subject, let's sit down a minute and discuss the issue."

So the old men sat on Ray's woodpile and Ray continued, "You know the doctor ordered me to stay out of the woods this fall. He wants me to have my heart operation before deer season. But you know that has to wait. One more season in the woods won't hurt."

"Yes, but you know I agree with your doctor. I can't see what that has to do with the little Winchester," Archie commented.

"Well, as you shoot left-handed this .30-30 is just the rifle for you. And then you can join me back there in the woods on the first day," Ray told his old friend. "I'll load up some good accurate rounds for you and perhaps you will bag the Big One."

Archie sat quiet for a few minutes. Ray knew that this was not the time to push with more questions, or comments.

Finally, Archie started to talk. It all seemed to come out at once. "Ray, you're my friend and I'm glad we came home to enjoy our last years together. But now you insist on acting stupidly. There will be many more deer seasons. What if you have to give up one to insure you will be here to enjoy others? No, I'm not going to play a role in making it easier for you to violate your doctor's orders."

Ray sat stunned for several minutes. He knew Archie was right. However, that didn't change his mind.

"Arch, I'm going to go hunting the first two days. After that I will be ready to go to the hospital."

"I'll do the best I can to keep track of you from up here," Archie said.

The night before deer season found three of Ray's sons in a trailer house on a piece of property Randy had leased for deer hunting. Ray's oldest son now lived in Florida and couldn't make it home to hunt deer. The men had enjoyed a good supper. Randy was an excellent cook, having learned in the Army.

As they sat around the small stove used to heat the trailer, Andy said, "Dad called me last week to tell me he had loaded me some shells for the deer season. When I told him I would come down to pick them up, he asked me to bring the .30-30 down to him."

"What's up?" John asked, "does he plan to hunt with it?"

"I don't know," Randy responded. "But the last time I talked to him, I told him about your new rifle, Andy, and he told me that maybe he would ask you to bring the old rifle down to him."

"Well, I took it down as he thinks he can get Archie to hunt with him. You know Archie shoots left-handed and will have no trouble with the Model 94." Andy responded and added, "The old rifle means a lot to him. You know that all four of us shot our first bucks with it and it still shoots pretty good."

"I know the old man had something on his mind, but he didn't say anything even after I asked if everything was OK," Randy added. "You know when he decides something you can't change his mind, so I didn't try."

The men sat silent for some time. All were thinking about their father and the good hunts they had enjoyed together over the years. Most of these were during the years they were young boys growing up. Only Randy hunted with him regularly in recent years. He had an English Setter and Ray enjoyed watching the dog work. Finally Randy broke the silence.

"This is the last time I'm going to hunt with you guys during the deer season until Dad is gone. He just shouldn't hunt alone anymore."

"That probably is a good idea," John commented, "we can even take turns, unless the old man figures out what's up."

With that the conversation turned to other things, such as where each would stand the next morning. They all knew that if their dad were in camp, they would have been in bed hours ago.

And that's exactly where Ray was, sound asleep in his own bed with Rex snuggled down on his rug at the foot of the bed. Ray's hunting clothes were neatly piled on the bed in the spare bedroom. Rex knew he would have to hold down the fort by himself for a few days, while his master went forth to chase those trash game animals.

Ray got up early the next morning — opening day. He fried bacon and eggs, made some toast, and washed everything down with two cups of black coffee. He had packed a big lunch the night before and now filled his thermos bottle. He looked outside before dressing. It had snowed about two inches and the temperature stood at twenty-six degrees.

"Better put on some extra clothes," he thought.

He left the house at 6:15am and headed off for his blind. Yes, he carried the old .30-30. He also had twelve rounds of ammunition that he had hand loaded only a few days ago. This was the load he always loaded for Andy. He used RP cases with WLR primers. The powder was 33.5 grains of IMR 4831. The bullets were Hornady flat points. You have to use the flat point bullet in the Model 94.

On the way to the blind, Ray thought about Archie. He wished he were with him, carrying the old .30-30. But that would have to be another opening morning. In less than twenty minutes Ray was in his blind. First, he lit the lantern and then loaded his rifle. He now settled down to wait the dawn. He had spent over sixty years doing exactly the same thing at exactly the same time on November 15. Although an old man, Ray felt the excitement of the moment. He was as intense as always. Only five rounds were in the old rifle, one in the chamber and four in the magazine. The Model 94 had a habit of pushing bullets down into the cases if you filled it to capacity. Ray taught his boys that if they couldn't hit deer with five shots they would not hit them at all. He was never wrong.

The first light of day started to appear in the east. The snow took on a special glow as the light started to trickle in through the trees. Ray thought about the million other Michigan hunters who were also waiting for this magic moment. He smiled as he recalled how all deer hunters hope for snow, but when it comes many of them stay inside waiting for a better day.

"There are a lot more hunters out in the woods on nice days," he thought.

As the first hour of daylight slipped by and no deer had come by the blind, Ray knew it was unlikely that any deer were still out in the rye field. Actually it was now an oat field, seeded down to alfalfa for a future hay crop. It still would produce good deer pasture. He and Archie had checked the field three days earlier. Lots of deer were using the field and among the numerous tracks they picked out one animal that they were convinced was the Big One.

"He will make a mistake yet," Ray thought. "I hope I will be around long enough to get a chance at him. But if not me, I hope Archie will get him."

He now knew he only had a few years left. He thought about his doctor's orders not to hunt deer this fall. He was hopelessly addicted, so he waited.

Along with the first hour of good light came the rifle fire. Most of the shots up to now had been far off. It appeared to be a slow opening morning. Then two shots rang out back by the railroad grade. Ray knew the young hunter from Farwell would be on that stand. He hoped the young man had bagged a good buck, even the Big One. What a thrill that would be for him. It wasn't the Big One. The kid had just bagged his first buck, a fat four pointer.

Other than those shots, it was a quiet opener. Even the squirrels stayed in their nests. Ray stayed in his blind all day and didn't see a deer until just before dark. Then he heard the brush cracking down in the swamp southeast of the blind. A doe and two fawns came out of the swamp and worked their way around Ray and headed off toward the oat field.

"They will have to dig down through the soft snow to get their supper tonight," Ray thought.

When Ray left the blind a few minutes later, he headed out toward the east, the same way he had come in that morning. He didn't want to disturb the feeding deer that he knew were now in the field.

Archie had a good meal prepared for the returning hunter. And as soon as Ray turned on his yard light the phone rang.

"Come and get it," his old friend said.

"I'll be there as soon as I can get these heavy clothes off and change into something more appropriate," Ray replied.

He quickly mixed a drink and sipped on it as he changed into lighter clothes.

The second day was even quieter than the first. Ray got to the blind well before daylight, but he didn't see a single deer all morning. At noon he returned to the house for lunch. This was a major change in his hunting tactics. He knew that to be a successful deer hunter, you had to stay in the woods. However, failing to pack a lunch and going back to the house became routine. Also, he took the direct route. Head straight north to the lopped fencerow. Go through the fence where the old apple tree had stood and set a straight line across the old field to the house. Even though the weather remained nasty, with wind and snow every day, he often flushed ruffed grouse from under the fallen trees in the fencerow. And, of course, cottontail tracks were everywhere.

At noon on the fourth day of the season, Ray had seen only six deer in three and a half days of hunting. All had been does and fawns. He had forgotten his promise to Archie that he would only hunt two days.

"Oh well, maybe the good Lord knows I don't have any business dragging out a buck," he thought as he left the blind and headed home for lunch.

As he climbed through the fencerow tangle he noticed a movement on the edge of the brush, just southwest of the house. The old hunter froze, right on the field edge of the fencerow, and watched. A single deer left the brush and headed straight toward Ray across the semi-open field. It carried its head low and just trotted along toward the waiting hunter, who knew that it was likely a buck but he still couldn't see antlers. He watched the deer approach as it picked its way around small clumps of sumac, thornapple, and witch hazel. When the deer was about a hundred yards away, the old hunter saw the spikes.

"Here comes our winter meat supply," he thought.

When the buck was about sixty yards away Ray cocked the Model 94 and carefully raised it to his shoulder. The deer saw the movement and stopped and looked directly at the hunter. The flat nosed 170-grain bullet hit the buck just below the white spot on its neck. The spike horn didn't know what hit him and he fell dead in his tracks. Archie heard the shot and came back across the field to help dress out the animal. He then returned to his house for the four-wheeler to bring out the deer. An hour later the men were sitting at Ray's kitchen table enjoying a bowl of chili that Ray had cooked up the night before. It was made with canned venison from last year's deer and was excellent. The spike horn hung in Ray's garage.

"Our supply of canned venison is getting in short supply, so we better can some of this one," the old hunter told his friend. "Let's eat out tonight to celebrate another successful deer season."

Ray suggested they leave early, so they could stop at Jay's, the large sporting goods store north of Clare.

"Just so we can browse around a little," he told Archie.

At five o'clock the men were at Jay's, looking at the large assortment of hunting and fishing equipment.

"It sure is nice to see a store that features guns and hunting stuff without hiding the equipment in the back room or worse yet, not carrying anything of interest to hunters," Ray commented.

Archie noticed that Ray bought a second buck license before leaving the store for the restaurant. Of course, Ray knew that

Archie had a deer license as it came with the senior hunt license. Ray wanted to apply more pressure on his friend to get him to go hunting with him, but he didn't think that now was the time. Ray didn't know that his friend had almost broken down this fall, as he didn't want his friend to hunt alone. He had discussed the problem with Randy. Undoubtedly, that's what led up to Randy's announcement at his deer camp. Ray hadn't told his sons about delaying heart surgery.

It was well after dark when the old men left Doherty's and headed home. Archie had driven, as was his practice when eating at a place that served liquor. When they reached Archie's driveway he continued down the road toward Ray's place.

"Hey I can walk that short distance," Ray hollered at his old friend.

Too late, so Archie just ignored the comment. Just as he started to make the swing into Ray's driveway, he stopped the car. He had noticed deer eyes shining along the south side of the road, near the bottom of the clay hill. Right on Ray's prepared deer runway. As the men watched a huge buck crossed the road, right in the headlights. He had his nose to the ground and simply trotted across, heading north. "The Big One!" they both shouted at the same time. It was by far the largest deer either man had ever seen. They both had a good look at the buck. It was the first time they had seen him up so close. And the first time they saw him this year. He carried at least a ten-point rack, with a huge spread. The tines on the antlers were very long and appeared evenly spaced. Even in the car's headlights both men noticed the large antler bases.

"He is truly a Boone and Crockett buck," Ray thought.

Both men were very excited.

And when Ray told Archie, "Come on in, we've got to talk about this," Archie didn't object.

The first thing Ray did after entering the house was to turn on his NOAA scanner, which gives continuous weather broadcasts.

"Heavy snow warning in effect. Snow to start near daylight and continue for two days. This will be a major winter storm," the announcer said.

"What's the Big One doing clear up here from Deadman Swamp during the deer season, especially with a bad storm coming in?" Archie asked.

"Well, you know, I haven't been seeing a lot of deer. With the big acorn crop we have this fall I think most of the deer are still up in the oaks, by the firetower hill, digging down through the snow for acorns," Ray replied.

Both men knew that wildlife always took advantage of the good food source provided by the acorns and it took a lot of snow to chase deer to the swamp under those circumstances.

"Well, Ray continued, "I think the Big One just got lonesome back there in the swamp and decided to make a night of it up in the oak ridges, chasing the does."

Ray's explanation wasn't far from the truth. He knew the big deer covered several square miles during the breeding season.

"Although the rut is winding down, he just wanted to make the rounds one more time," Ray added.

"Tomorrow is the day we prove to him that he made a mistake," Ray said.

"You mean that we stand a good chance to ambush him on the way back to the swamp?" Archie asked.

Ray smiled widely at his friend's question. Seeing the big

buck had pushed him over the edge. He would join the next day's hunt. So Ray outlined a plan.

"This big storm will chase most deer out of the hills and they will head back to the shelter of the swamp. I'm betting that most of the movement will occur right after daylight and that our big buck will be among the does and fawns when they make the trip. And you know we have the best runway, right in our back-yard. I can't cover the whole runway system from my blind, as you know that many of the deer will split off back there in the field," Ray said as he gestured toward the small field where he had bagged the buck earlier in the day.

"Some will turn west and cross right by my blind. Others will veer off to the east and enter the woods near the east end of our lopped fencerow," Ray added.

"With two hunters we will see most of the deer headed for the swamp. I'd be happy to let you choose which stand you want. But the one standing in the southeast corner of the field should hide in the fencerow and be prepared to shoot the deer in the field, because once they enter the woods they will escape," Ray told his new deer hunting friend.

Ray was surprised and pleased when Archie replied, "OK, I'll stand on the east end of the fencerow and you go back to your heated blind. You have no business even hunting, and standing out there in the open field will be tough with the weather we expect tomorrow," Archie said.

Ray knew his old friend was right, so didn't put up an argu-ment.

"I'll wear my ice fishing clothes and if I get too cold I can always return to the house," Archie said.

So the ambush was planned, except for firearms.

"You knew why I had Andy return the .30-30, and it was exactly for this reason. You shoot left-handed and my bolt action rifles are all right-handed. Why don't you take the Model 94 and I'll hunt with the .30-06," Ray offered.

"No thanks. I've got a handful of rifled slugs for the Sweet Sixteen and I'll just carry it. Besides, I'm shooting quite well now and I know I can knock one over if I get the chance," Archie replied.

Ray agreed as he had watched Archie steadily improve since they started to hunt together again. Also, he had bagged his first three bucks with 16-gauge slugs and he knew the new slugs were even more accurate, up to sixty yards or more.

So the men headed toward their own beds and both dreamed of having the Big One in their sights. Ray was sleepless and did a lot of tossing and turning. His mind was on the next day. He knew they were right on the best runway between where the deer were feeding and the shelter of the big swamp. And tomorrow the severe storm would certainly have the deer moving. The situation was nearly perfect.

Early the next morning the old men headed back for the woods to put their plan in effect. The lantern Ray carried to heat his blind cast a light glow on the snow as they headed across the field to the spot Archie would stand. Ray wanted to make sure Archie was in the right spot. Archie carried Lew's old semi-automatic shotgun and Archie noticed that Ray had stuck with the Model 94. When they reached the east end of the lopped fencerow, Ray helped Archie prepare a stand that would mostly hide the hunter from approaching deer and still offer open shooting in that corner of the field. There was a clump of sumac and thornapple bushes growing in the fence line between their properties, so the men had to break off a few branches that might deflect a slug.

"If a buck comes along the fence on your property, just shoot before he gets behind that tangle," Ray advised.

Archie knew what his friend meant. A bullet or rifled slug would have a tough time plowing through that dense brush.

The promised snow then started to fall. From the forecast they knew they were in for a real blinger. A light breeze blew out of the east. Just the right direction to bring a heavy snow. Neither man knew that what was coming would be a record snowfall for November in their area. And that would be added to the four inches already on the ground.

"Well, good luck, old friend," Ray said as he disappeared in the falling snow toward his blind.

As he walked through the woods to the blind, he had a couple sharp pains in his chest.

"Gas pains, again," he thought.

And he just brushed it off in the excitement of the moment. When he reached the blind he crawled over the entrance and brushed the snow off his Hotseat and milk carton. After placing the lantern in the corner of the blind he sat down on his stool and loaded the little rifle. One cartridge went in the chamber and the hammer lowered to half cock, the .30-30's safety. Four more rounds were pushed into the tubular magazine. Ray knew the rifle would hold seven, but five it was.

He then settled down to wait the dawn. He felt more excitement than even on opening day. He felt confident that they had at last cut the Big One off from the safety of the big swamp. Sure, he might have gone back there before daylight. However, it had been a quiet deer season so far and perhaps the big buck would be careless due to lack of hunting pressure. It was snowing like mad and several times Ray had to brush the snow from the open sights on his rifle. He then placed the Model 94 under a pine slab that protruded into the blind. No more snow fell in the sights. Yet the hunter could instantly raise the firearm if a deer appeared.

Ray thought about another snowy morning, many years earlier. It was the third morning of the season and he had decided to take a stand a little nearer to his deer-hunting buddy, Dick. This blind was one that he and his friend had prepared for Dick's night stand and it was right on the edge of a big cedar swamp. His friend would probably have the first chance at bucks moving from their feeding area to the safety of the swamp as his favorite morning stand was only just a little over a quarter of a mile to the west. That didn't bother Ray, as deer often got by his friend.

"Be alert about 10:30 as I will walk over to see how you're doing. I'll cut through that stand of pines between us and chase one out to you," Dick told his hunting buddy.

They both got a laugh out of that, as they knew that deer hunting isn't such a sure thing.

Over the years Ray had chased several bucks out to Dick and he had bagged about half of them. So Ray snuggled down in Dick's blind and waited for daylight. Nothing was moving and the snow kept falling on his rifle scope, so he carefully placed the .243 under a pine slab much like the one that now sheltered the .30-30, as he waited for the Big One. As he waited he got cold. It was a bitter cold morning. He stood up to get his circulation going and as it was only a little after nine o'clock, he was facing east watching the swamp edge. It was at least an hour before he had to start thinking about Dick's promised drive. There Ray stood, with his hands in his pockets trying to get them warmed up when he heard a twig snap behind him in the direction of his hunting partner.

"That can't be Dick," Ray thought.

So he carefully glanced back over his shoulder and there standing right in the open only seventeen yards from the blind stood a spikehorn.

The buck was staring right at the hunter and tucked away under the pine slab was Ray's rifle. To make matters worse he still had his gloved hands in his pockets. Talk about frustration! Ray knew the deer had spotted him and was just waiting for a movement before taking off in high gear. He did manage to get his hands out of his pockets and get one on the rifle before the buck bounded off. He managed to reach the aspen slash about fifty yards away before Ray got the rifle up. Now all he had to aim at was a fast disappearing white flag. A quick squint through the scope and the little .243 bullet was on its way. The buck collapsed in a heap. Ray still has the tanned hide. There are no bullet holes in it. Yes, that's where it was hit. Ray's punster friend said the bullet "wrecked-em." A few minutes after Ray shot the buck, Dick appeared out of the slashing. He got cold and made his little deer drive earlier than expected.

"Enough thinking about the old days," Ray now thought. "I better pay attention to the problem at hand."

The snow drifted down in sheets. You could even hear the heavy flakes as they drifted down through the oak leaves of a little oak that stood just a few feet from the blind. It still held its leaves. It was now full daylight and Ray glanced at his watch. It was a few minutes after eight o'clock. Meanwhile, Archie waited on the field edge. He was sitting on a small log that he and Ray had prepared for a stool. He wasn't yet cold as his ice fishing gear was high quality and managed to keep the warmth in and the cold out.

Just then the snow seemed to lift a little and Archie glancing off toward his house saw the Big One cross the road east of his house! It was about three-eighth of a mile from Archie to the deer. Yet, there was no question about what deer it was. Archie could feel his heart beating with the excitement of the moment.

"Leave it to that old buck to do the unexpected," he thought.

The big deer seemed to be in no hurry. He just trotted along holding his head and huge antlers near the ground as he made his way toward the big swamp. At first Archie thought the buck would continue on and cross east of him too far away for a shot. When the deer turned west and headed toward the duck pond he thought it would bed down in the marsh grass and cattails on the pond's edge. But he didn't. When the Big One cut around the southeast end of the pond and headed right at the hunter, Archie's heart almost stopped. The old hunter hunkered down behind the brush that helped hide him and waited. Now the buck was just east of the fence and moving toward the south and it was obvious that he would shortly be within easy shooting distance. Archie knew that with a rifle in Ray's hands the prize trophy would already be on the ground. Now the shotgun seemed inadequate for the task at hand. Archie remembered that he had to shoot before the buck got behind the brush in the fencerow, but he waited until the deer was less than fifty yards away.

Meanwhile, Ray sat in his blind and waited. He watched a big doe come from the north and cross just east of him. It entered the swamp to the southeast about where the six-pointer had after being hit by Ray's bullet a year ago. Just as the doe entered the thicket, Ray heard Archie's shotgun boom.

He sat still for a minute then thought, "Only one shot. A good sign. I pray that he just got the Big One."

However, all wasn't well with the other hunter. Just as Archie raised his gun the big buck saw a movement. He reacted immediately. He didn't stop and look, like so many younger bucks do. His first leap took him fifteen feet to the south. Archie's slug caught him in the big bound, but it hit about ten inches too far back. As the deer had still been approaching, the slug tore through the buck just missing the vital chest cavity. It angled back and stopped just under the deer's hide on the far side, just in front of the left hind leg.

If Archie had Ray's long hunting experience he would have noticed a slight stumble from the big deer when the slug hit him. Unfortunately, he didn't. Archie had no chance for a second shot as the deer ran to the south, completely hidden by the brushy fencerow. If Archie had made a mistake it was his failure to get his shotgun up a little earlier. Perhaps when the big deer had his head behind a bush or tree, but he didn't, and even Ray could have made the same mistake. Only Ray would have been shooting a rifle that would have left holes on both sides of the animal.

Ray knew he should wait until his friend came down to his blind with the news. There was still a chance that Archie had missed and the buck might still be between them. So he remained alert and watched. He was aware that the snow continued to build up and now covered everything with a thick blanket.

As soon as the buck disappeared to the south, Archie left his stand and climbed over the fence to investigate. He was sure he had missed, but he had to make sure. He followed the buck's trail along the east side of the fence for almost a hundred yards. There the deer jumped the fence and headed west, directly toward Ray's blind. Archie waited there for several minutes, expecting to hear Ray's shot. When it didn't come he climbed back over the fence and followed the trail for another hundred yards, carefully looking for blood but not expecting any. Already the trail was rapidly being filled in by the heavy snowfall.

Archie was now completely convinced that he had missed the big buck. He thought about checking in with Ray, but decided against it when he thought there might be a chance that the deer was still waiting out there for another deer to accompany him to the swamp. No need to mess up Ray's hunt. So, with great disappointment, he turned and headed back to his house. He could tell his friend the story later. Little did he know that a high-power rifle bullet would have passed clear through the big buck leaving clear evidence of a hit. Then the hunter could have tracked down the wounded animal.

Shortly after Archie had returned to his house, Ray could stand the suspense no longer. He had to check up on his old friend. He left the blind and headed off to the east toward the line fence, his usual route to the blind in the morning. There was about a foot of snow on the ground and it was still snowing like there was no tomorrow. Just fifty yards from the north/south fence he cut the tracks of the Big One. The deer was running hard with no sign of any injuries.

"So, Archie missed," Ray thought.

He backtracked the big buck toward Archie's stand.

Suddenly he stopped. There, clearly smeared on a small red maple sapling, was some blood from the deer. Ray knew the buck had brushed against the small tree in his mad dash for the big swamp.

"He's hit on the right side," Ray thought.

He continued on toward his friend's stand to give him the news. He was sure that Archie didn't know he had hit the deer or he would still be on the trail. Ray found a few drops of blood spattered on a small aspen shoot, but nothing more. Shortly, Ray came to Archie's tracks in the snow and he was aware that his friend had followed the big buck for some distance before deciding that he had missed the animal. Now Ray was sure that his friend wouldn't still be on his stand. And he was right. Archie's tracks headed off toward his house. It was obvious that he had been gone for some time as his tracks were almost completely snowed in.

Ray started toward the house to get his old friend, but stopped when he realized that by the time they returned the big buck's tracks would be snowed in and they would not be able to trail him. He realized that the job was now his responsibility, so he turned and soon took up the trail of the wounded animal. Even though Ray was an experienced tracker the first quarter-mile of the trail was very difficult. Snow had eliminated all signs of blood and only an occasional sapling told Ray he was following the right deer. Fortunately he didn't cross the trail of the big doe, or any other deer, which would have confused any tracker. Sometimes, Ray had to get down almost on his knees to peer ahead to find the trail in the deep snow. Snow had caved in on the tracks in many places and a lesser man would have given up and returned to the warmth of his house. Not Ray.

Finally, Ray found where the Big One had entered the low-land brush swamp on the north side of the railroad grade. Under the screen of the few big cedar trees the old hunter found clear tracks made by the big deer. If he had any doubts about the buck he followed, they were now erased. No other deer made such tracks in the snow. When the buck passed through a dense clump of cedars that held up most of the new snow, a clear blood trail was evident. Ray now knew that the slug had not gone clear through the deer, which made trailing much more difficult.

"I'm going to track down this magnificent animal or die try-ing," Ray vowed to himself.

The buck continued on toward the big swamp, through the densest part of the lowland brush north of the tracks. Ray moved carefully along the trail, with the heavy snow dampen-ing the sound of the hunter. He often stopped and watched ahead as best he could. As the swamp conifers held up most of the new snow, it was much easier to stay on the trail. Yet Ray knew that if the deer were still in the open, his trail would be impossible to follow. Snow fell off the trees on the old hunter and it wasn't long before Ray could feel water trickling down his neck from melting snow that had managed to get down the neck of his coat. He had to stop to raise the hood on his deer-hunting coat. He hated that hood, as it shut off his hearing and much of his vision, but now it became a necessity. He knew he wouldn't hear the deer when he jumped him in this dense thick-et. If he didn't stop here, north of the railroad grade, Ray knew he would lose the trail when he crossed the aspen ridge just north of the grade.

Finally, in desperation, Ray had to stop to clean his glasses.

They were wet and covered with snow that just about blocked his ability to see the trail. In spite of his years Ray could see pretty well without his glasses, so he folded them up and put them in his coat pocket. Ray knew he should stop and take a breather. He could feel the effects of this vigorous work. His old heart was clearly sending him a message to give up the chase, but his mind kept urging him on.

"Perhaps a lesser buck could be forgotten," Ray thought.

But, deep down, his psychological make-up wouldn't permit him to give up, even for a spikehorn. All efforts must be made to recover any wounded game animal. He knew that the same ethics flowed through the veins of almost all hunters of his generation.

As Ray stood there in the swamp adjusting his hood and folding his glasses, he heard the brush cracking about fifty yards ahead. He knew the Big One had left his bed. After pulling the hood over his head Ray moved ahead to investigate. Although he knew there was no chance of seeing the buck in this thick cover, he was now encouraged because he knew he would be able to follow the fresh trail through the open aspen stand. Sure enough, there in the snow under the cedars was a huge deer bed. The buck had been there within fifteen minutes from the time of Archie's shot. Ray glanced at his watch. It was now a quarter to one. If he had waited any longer before checking up on his old friend, the big buck would have certainly been lost. Perhaps he would get away now, but at any rate old Ray would give him his best effort. He now had a fresh trail to follow and he knew that in spite of the snow coming down in blankets, he would not lose it. Ray studied the bed and judged the deer to be badly wounded.

"If I can just keep going, I'll have this deer before dark," he thought.

Ray knew that all other hunters had beaten a hasty retreat to their homes, motels, cabins, or trailers. There was no chance of chasing the wounded deer past anyone else, so the job of recovering the animal fell only on his shoulders. So there he was, one old man against the wits of one old, wise white-tailed buck. In a way the odds were even. The deer was badly wounded and the old man was dying from a bad heart.

Ray knew that neither would live to see another day unless he could end the chase within the next couple hours. He had won many such contests in the past and now was confident of the outcome of this one. He stopped and prayed to God for strength before setting out on the fresh blood trail, now clearly defined in the new fallen snow. The buck left the little swamp and cut across the aspen ridge and went over the grade right on the historic crossing east of the big cut.

When Ray reached the grade about fifteen minutes behind the deer, the snow had already covered up the blood sign. Only an occasional drop or two on saplings that stood above the rapidly deepening snow insured the old hunter that he was on the right trail. The big deer had not run more than 200 yards after leaving his bed before he settled down to an easy lope toward the big swamp. He stopped on the knoll north of the grade and watched up and down the right-of-way. When he crossed over he went full speed in big bounds. Any hunter guarding that runway would have had a hard time hitting the running buck. When Ray reached that spot, he knew why the Big One had lived so long.

Ray stood on the grade and looked south. He now knew that

the contest would be won or lost in the big swamp. Then he took up the trail again. The big deer quit running when he entered the heavy cover offered by the swamp conifers. He then started to walk. When Ray entered the swamp on the trail he knew that the buck had gained several minutes on him, but he didn't worry. The blood trail was clearly evident to the old hunter, as the cedars held up much of the new snow. Again, he had to adjust the hood on his coat. He wondered how a deer with such large antlers could negotiate his way through the dense swamp.

His mind went back to a time he stood on an aspen ridge in the elk country. He and a hunting club manager were searching for a sick cow elk. His partner was several hundred yards away when he jumped a huge bull elk. It headed straight to Ray. Ray could hear the bull coming a long time before it came in sight. The bull carried his huge rack laid back on his shoulders; they were crashing into the trees on either side of his body and making a real racket. The bull's big body smashed down any small trees that got in his way.

"Sounded like a freight train approaching," he later told the manager of Canada Creek Club.

The bull crossed only fifty yards south of where Ray stood. He still treasures that experience. And to think that many area folks then thought that all of Michigan's elk were as tame as cattle.

The Big One hadn't gone far into the swamp, before he reached the small feeder stream that enters Deadman Lake on the northwest side. The flowing water was barely visible under the deep snow. He didn't cross the stream, but turned east toward the lake. After following the stream for a little ways, he crossed the footpath that Ray and Archie used to reach the lake.

He crossed that in one bound and turned northerly until he reached a dense stand of cedars. He was now truly in the big swamp that had been his sanctuary for much of his life.

It wouldn't be that way today. On his trail came one of the most experienced deer hunters in the state of Michigan. Certainly, Ray was old and in poor physical condition, but, the old hunter knew every trick in the books about how to outwit white-tailed bucks. However, Ray knew he had no business following the wise old deer into the interior of the big swamp. He knew he might not come out, but his hunting instincts drove him on. His old heart was working as hard as possible and telling him all about it. At times a sharp pain would shoot up his left arm.

"Got those gas pains again from not eating any lunch," Ray lied to himself, "I should have put a sandwich in my pocket when I left the blind."

The old man was then standing on the little footpath. He again removed his coat hood and shook the snow off it. He also cleaned the snow off the little Model 94 and squinted through the peep sights. The big square front sight showed up plainly in the old man's field of vision.

"I'm sure glad I'm carrying this rifle today. I know I can hit him if he gives me half a chance," Ray thought.

When the old hunter reached the spot where the Big One turned off toward the north he thought the big deer was preparing to bed down again. And he was right. However, the deer had already left his bedding spot in the dense cedars, when he heard Ray on his trail. He cut to the southeast toward the north end of the lake. When Ray entered the dense thicket he soon came to the vacated bedding site. The old hunter studied the sign left in the packed snow. He concluded that the buck's strength was ebbing. Otherwise the old deer would have continued moving in the swamp to put more distance between himself and his pursuer.

"I don't think he will go far before laying down again," Ray thought. "Won't Archie be pleased when I tell him that he bagged the Big One? He might even have a drink with me to celebrate."

When the deer reached the north end of the little lake, it turned south along the east side of the lake. Obviously, the wounded-buck found the going a little easier after passing through a dense stand of alder and willow. It now took a route through the marsh grass and cattails right on the lake's edge. And as Ray had predicted, the deer again started to look for another bedding spot. Ray knew that if the deer continued along the lake for another quarter mile, it would reach a small area completely covered with cattail. The Big One had often bedded there before. If the deer could just reach that spot he would just lay up and wait for the hunter to approach. Then a few big bounds would again put him in a dense cedar stand where he would have another chance to stay ahead of his trailer. He feared the old hunter on his trail. Lesser men would have given up long before now.

But Ray was back there, just plodding along, and watching here and there for any sign of movement. He knew the end was in sight, so he would stop often to plot his next move. As the trail turned south along the lake's edge, Ray knew exactly where the big buck was headed.

"He just made his last mistake," the old hunter thought.

With that knowledge Ray stopped following the deer's trail.

He got out his compass, a Silva Ranger, like the one he had carried since 1949. The first one had belonged to the State of Michigan and he had to turn it in when he retired. He bought this one shortly after retiring.

"If you ever use one, you will never go back to anything else," he often told his friends.

He now ran a compass line straight east through the swamp conifers for a quarter mile. Then he turned straight south until he broke out on the aspen/birch ridge on the southeast corner of the lake. He then turned west toward the lake. Now he proceeded with great caution. Just a few steps and then stand for a couple minutes before repeating the procedure. As he waited he again became more aware of how severe this snowstorm had become. The wind had switched around to the northwest and was picking up in velocity.

"You just don't notice it down there in the cedars," he thought.

About twenty minutes later, he stood on the lakeshore. He had succeeded in encircling the Big One, as his tracks had not crossed Ray's calculated entrapment.

"Now I know exactly where you are," Ray thought.

He stood still for several minutes before starting his stalk. He needed the breather. Severe pain now radiated up his left arm and into the shoulder area. Also, the old hunter was aware of stabbing chest pains. Now he didn't try to deny the cause. He just ignored it. The moment at hand was primary.

Ray looked at his watch; it was 2:30. He knew that Archie would be worried about his failure to come in for lunch.

"He's probably back there in my blind checking up on me," Ray thought. "Well, hang on old friend, I'm about ready to finish off your big buck."

He looked north along the lake's shore. On the edge of the water was the cattail clump that Ray knew was there. It was just over a hundred yards from where he stood. The old hunter was reasonably sure that the big buck had bedded down in those cattails. And he was right. Now Ray called up all the knowledge he had filed away in his brain about deer and deer hunting. First, he cleared all the snow from his rifle and made sure the peep sight was open. He used his red hanky. It could dry off later. Then he turned the hood on his coat all the way down and out of his way. He raised his rifle and quickly sighted on several objects near at hand. Sort of like shadow boxing. He was now ready for the stalk of his lifetime.

"It's now or never," he told himself.

Then he started his stalk. One step, then wait a full minute before taking another. Look ahead to where you plan to place your next footprint, then move ahead another step. The little rifle was held at ready. Another step and another wait.

"If that old buck is not there, I'll sure feel foolish," Ray told himself.

Ray didn't have to worry about that, he was. Ray noted that the wind was just right.

"That old buck will never know I'm on this side of him until I'm practically standing on him."

A half-hour elapsed with the stalk going as planned.

Ray was now only twenty yards from his objective. He moved ahead another two steps with the required wait in between. Suddenly, the Big One heard the snow crunch under Ray's foot. He jumped to his feet in one big bound toward the cedars. He had hardly moved before the 170-grain rifle bullet caught him, right in the side of the neck. Down he went, almost in the bed he had just left. The old hunter had done his job.

A warm glow coursed through Ray's body. He had experienced it before on numerous occasions, when he had bagged lesser bucks. He had spent years trying to figure out why it came at a time like this. His best guess was that it had something to do with the dark past, when all of his ancestors were hunters.

It seemed to say, "There will be joy in our camp tonight. Everyone will eat."

Ray accepted the fact that it must have been a wonderful feeling then, as it is now. Ray walked up to the fallen trophy. Its huge antlers pushed up almost to the top of the cattails. He counted the points. Twelve. Six on each side. All the points were long and heavy. The main beams swung out to form a tremendous spread, with huge antler bases. Ray turned the head up and cradled the Model 94 across the rack. He knew the little rifle was thirty-eight inches long. Only four or five inches protruded on each side of the antlers. About a thirty-inch spread.

"This buck is truly a Boone and Crockett record for this county," Ray thought.

The excitement had deadened Ray's pain. Now it came back in all its fury. He began to wonder if he could make it back. He knew the heavy snow had dampened the rifle shot. There would be no way for Archie to hear it even if he were standing in Ray's blind. There would be no sign of any tracks north of the railroad grade. The snow had taken care of that.

Then Ray, overcome with the emotions of the moment, did something he had never done before. With his right hand on the rifle still cradled across the Big One's antlers, and his left hand on one of the big tines on the left antler, Ray fell to his knees and prayed to God.

"First, I want to thank you for giving me the strength and ability to follow the trail and end the suffering of this magnificent animal. We hunters truly regret that we are not perfect predators. I understand that Your plan for man's domination over lesser species did not overlook the possibility of these things happening. Perhaps it is part of your plan to make us realize that, although created in Your image, we are not perfect. Sometimes, when we are aware of these defects, like now, it is difficult to bear. Please forgive us and help future hunters to better understand that they are part of Your plan to fulfill Your will.

"I want to thank You for making it possible for the natural environment, that You planned for the enjoyment and nourishment of Your children, to produce such a magnificent animal as this buck. I pray that his progeny will continue to fulfill their role by passing on his superior genes to future generations of white-tailed deer.

"I want to thank You for the enjoyment the natural world has given me all these years I have been here on Your earth. The lakes, forests, rivers, and yes even these wonderful swamps, You provided have been deeply appreciated. And although I spent all of my life trying to unravel Your secrets regarding Nature, forgive me for not being wiser. I pray that I have left behind some ideas that more intelligent humans can build on to insure the future survival of Your Natural world. Please grant those who follow the necessary tools and intelligence to do a better job in protecting and understanding the natural environment of this wonderful planet.

"Now, if it is Your will, please give me the strength to return to my home and bring the good news to my dear friend, Archie. AMEN."

When the prayer was finished Ray stayed on his knees for a moment before rising. He looked through the cattails to the edge of the lake, less that fifty feet away. The lake had not yet frozen and the northwest wind gently lapped the waves against the shore. He could see the nearest white birches, their branches swaying in the freshening breeze. Over all the landscape lay a blanket of pure white snow. More snow was coming across the lake in sheets and gently falling to the ground next to Ray and The Big One.

"It truly is a beautiful world you gave Your children, God."

With that thought, Ray shifted his weight to his left foot and started to rise. He was aware of a strange, dark cloud that gradually fell over his world. He fell forward in the snow beside the Big One.

The heavy snow soon covered both bodies.

Appendix

The Conservator   **Spring 1988 Edition**

From the President's pen

On Saturday, February 13, I had the pleasure of representing the Michigan Conservation Foundation at a one day meeting called by Karl Hosford, Chief, Wildlife Division, Michigan Department of Natural Resources. The purpose of the meeting was to discuss "how state, federal, and private organizations can cooperate in achieving wetland habitat goals in Michigan." The Wildlife Division distributed a listing of 53 projects where private funds are needed to meet habitat objectives. I'm sure that with your assistance, the *Michigan Conservation Foundation* can help with some of these projects.

The significance of this meeting was that it brought numerous organizations together in an attempt to coordinate activities to meet a common goal: wetland preservation, restoration, and development. Frankly, I was amazed at the number of private organizations represented. I've been around the conservation movement for 45 years,

and I didn't know some of these organizations even existed. I want to list them for you—remember, these are only organizations interested in waterfowl and wetlands (I'll list them in the order registered at the meeting): Michigan Waterfowl Association; Waterfowl U.S.A.; *Michigan Conservation Foundation;* Michigan Great Lakes Wildlife Festival: Interlake Chapter Waterfowl U.S.A.; Ducks Unlimited; Shiawassee Citizens and Hunters Association; Michigan Wildlife Habitat Foundation; Michigan Duck Hunters Association; and the Michigan Audubon Society.

If I didn't miss anyone, that's a dozen private organizations. In addition, the following public agencies were represented: The Wildlife Division (DNR); the U.S. Forest Service (Huron-Manistee and Hiawatha); U.S. Fish and Wildlife Service; and Central Michigan University.

Now if anyone doubts that citizens of Michigan are concerned about our wetlands and waterfowl resources, they'd better think again. These people are dedicated and organized to protect the values they believe in.

Some question the need for so many separate groups, all working for essentially the same cause. Please count me as a supporter of all of the organizations standing up and fighting to preserve Michigan's wildlife resources. This is a grassroots movement; and if many organizations are more efficient, so be it!

As you know, I believe the *Michigan Conservation Foundation* can do a better job through local chapters. Most people are willing to invest time and money into projects that affect their local interest.

Our Chapter Organization Committee (Earnest Marenich , chairperson), has completed the guidelines for chapter organizations. It's an excellent piece of work.

I recommend that we proceed!

Raymond D. Schofield

President

Winter 1989 Edition   The Conservator

From the President's pen

Stakes high in Baiting Game

To bait or not to bait. Ah, that is the question. Or is it?

Actually, the crux of this column is not to paraphrase Will Shakespeare. Nor is it to take issue with either faction in the argument of whether or not to bait game. Actually it is intended to address my fears over the pitting of hunter against hunter and, in so doing, supply major weaponry to those who would outlaw hunting altogether.

After more than half a century of hunting, I've asked myself, so many times, How did all this adversity in the brotherhood of hunters come about?

I can address this issue best as a deer hunter because that's an area where I'm well experienced. And while I personally don't believe baiting deer is necessary, even worthwhile, I'm not taking issue with those who do. Today a good number of deer hunters bait, including several good friends—and I don't consider them poor sportsmen!

Granted, when I began hunting, times were different. It was a wonderful time to take to the Michigan woods. Licenses were just two bits beyond two bucks, and the deer herd was in good shape. There where were only about a third of the sportsmen afield with whom to share the bucks, and hunters were welcome on all public and almost all private lands.

We were successful, however, not because deer hunting was easier, but because we taught ourselves about the behavior of deer under varying conditions and

attempted to bag our bucks where the chances of success appeared best. Our favorite deer stands were selected after much scouting and acquainting ourselves with the lay of the land. We taught ourselves about the natural movement of deer. No one, to my knowledge, baited.

Actually, I question that baiting during the firearms deer season is even worthwhile. During the archery season, I guess I can see some logic to it, primarily because archers tend to stay put. But, firearms hunters move about a great deal, and that results in deer being spooked past and into the rifle sights of those hunters with the required blend of stamina and patience.

In fact, hunter movement more often will keep deer away from, rather than bringing them to baited areas! When breeding and survival are foremost in the minds of these creatures, no amount of sugar beets, apples or carrots is going to "bring him in" to a stand.

One concern I have, however, is the possibility that baited areas can sometimes prove detrimental to the deer herd long after the long guns are back in the rack. Not all bait piles are consumed by November 30th—or, for that matter, by December 30th—and many are placed far from winter cover. Easy food sources can hold deer out of the yards too long, causing real hardship for fawns when the big blizzards hit in January. I've seen it happen!

Then should baiting be outlawed? Although I can opine without reservation that baiting isn't

essential to being successful, I firmly believe the question should remain a decision for the individual.

That being an unlikely alternative however,  I'll say there's one thing that could help ease tensions between the factions—to define exactly, What is baiting? Is baiting the hunting of areas filled with farm crops or strategically-placed rye fields? I hardly think so, for a firearms deer hunter would be foolish not to take advantage of natural deer movement to or away from such food sources. Yet without definition, any proposed anti-baiting legislation easily could prohibit exactly that. To the proponents of outlawing baiting, therefore, I ask that you at least clearly define what it is you intend to do away with.

Even if baiting is a matter of ethics, bitterly arguing who among us is the most ethical merely grows the trees that hide the forest. Let's not forget that a house divided against itself cannot stand; and that while we busy ourselves scrapping, antihunters are taking full advantage of the opportunity to remove the question from our hands altogether.

Rayme CH Schofield

President

Page 2   The Conservator   Late Winter 1990

From the President's pen

Let's have regulations that manage the resource

The 1989 firearm deer season is now history. Whether we hunters managed to harvest a record number of deer remains to be determined. It appears that a lot of deer were taken in spite of weather that ranged from good to bad to outright horrible. Isn't that the usual fare Mother Nature dishes out from November 15 to 30?

Opening day found me on the same popple island in the swamp that I hunted as a 14 year old boy in 1939 — 50 years ago. Not my favorite deer stand, but good enough to produce a buck on the first morning almost every year. This year was no exception — and there he was at 8:43 a.m. I hope your hunt was as exciting and successful.

The second buck license allows most successful hunters to continue to hunt, and that's one of the good changes made in the regulations during the past few years. For years I continued my deer hunting recreation with a camp deer license in my pocket (an extra buck deer for each group of four hunters hunting out of a camp). I find the extra buck license a satisfactory solution to the age-old problem of "party" hunting.

I'm a member of the old school that believes that the deer herd should provide *hunting recreation* and not just bucks or does lined up on the meat pole. I can be counted on to oppose any regulation that will "chase" successful hunters out of the woods. The bonus deer permit provided extra hunting recreation for successful hunters, although restricting hunting to a specific area. That's the story for 1989 — but what about the future?

I'm concerned that we deer hunters are facing increased regulations brought about by some *real and some imagined* problems. Let's not forget what happened to waterfowl hunting. Do we want regulations to chip away at our deer hunting freedoms until they "kill the goose that lays the golden egg?" Quote: "DNR estimates deer hunting worth $300 million annually!" — and don't forget that deer hunters provide the lion's share of game and fish revenues.

I hear "loose talk" coming from several sources about restricting buck hunting when studies show that the 1-1/2 year old bucks (fawns this year, 1-1/2's next fall) *"will get the job done."* And even in heavily hunted areas, a few bucks live to 2-1/2 and some to 3-1/2 years. I recall one buck coming out of Missaukee County that was aged at 6-1/2 years old!

Baiting bothers me, too, but it's too late to worry about it now. Arguments will only pit hunters against hunters, and we'll all end up losing. As I've said before, you don't have to bait to be successful. Of course, rye patches are used to concentrate deer in a specific area — a form  of baiting — but I can ethically accept farming for wildlife. I'd like to see baiting just go away, but it won't.

The "shining" law is now more restrictive than what I like, but as I no longer drive around after dark looking for deer, I can accept it. A lot of people enjoy looking at deer with spotlights, with no gun in the car, and they still can prior to November 1 (before 11:00 p.m.). But if on the way to deer camp a big buck crosses the road in your headlights, wouldn't you stop to look? You're guilty if you do. It's splitting hairs ... the trouble with restrictive laws.

This fall we lost another deer hunting freedom — every firearm must now be placed in a case or locked in the truck or other inaccessible place when transported in a vehicle. No longer can we simply take out the bolt or otherwise break down a firearm. I've always preferred a bolt action rifle for several reasons, not the least of which is the ease of removing the bolt to avoid putting a wet rifle in a case. Didn't your firearm get soaking wet opening day this year? If you hunt out of a pickup truck (and who doesn't?), what did you do? Return to camp with a wet gun in a wet case? A heck of a way to treat a faithful old firearm! Rust and "rain specking" sets in almost immediately.

And what about hunters who organize deer drives? They end up on the other end of the section with their

(Continued on page 5)

Late Winter 1990

New regs need thought first!

(continued from page 2)

cases back at the start. Remove the bolt and stay legal? No longer!

Now, really, what has that restriction got to do with managing the resource? Will we have more deer because we have to put our wet rifles in cases? Will it curtail illegal road hunting? I think not. I'll bet some hunters can get their rifles out of a case faster than I can get the bolt back in my Model 700 Remington. Unnecessary restriction? You bet.

Let's stop adding new laws to restrict our deer hunting freedoms. We should request that our regulators *always* ask, "Is this restriction *absolutely* essential for management of the resource?" If not, let's learn to live with a few imperfect laws. The deer herd has.☐

Raymond D. Schofield
President

Page 4   The Conservator   **Spring 1992**

Are we ready for "quality" bucks?

by Raymond D. Schofield

In the November 30, 1991 Venture Outdoors section of the Muskegon Chronicle, an article by Bob Gwizdz entitled "Hunters Target Bigger Bucks" quotes Ed Langenau, the Department of Natural Resources deer expert, as saying that hunters are starting to clamor for "quality deer management." This means larger-antlered bucks. Gwizdz wisely asks the question: "Is Michigan ready for quality buck management?"

Recently, I have noticed several articles in other publications advocating hunting regulations aimed at producing large-antlered deer. As no one has presented the other side, I think it's time someone answered Gwizdz's question with a resounding "NO!" It is my contention that most Michigan deer hunters are not willing to make the sacrifices necessary to initiate a quality buck program.

Let's look at the problems involved and see if you agree. First, only quality deer range is capable of producing big antlers on deer in a reasonable time frame. Winters are the bottleneck, and most Michigan deer-wintering areas are in poor condition. With few exceptions, only agricultural areas of the state provide adequate food for deer during this critical period.

Perhaps the most important problem, which I view as an unrealistic goal, is that hunters will have to put off harvesting small bucks, especially the 1-1/2- and 2-1/2-year-old animals These deer now make up the bulk of the annual buck harvest in most hunting areas.

What does this mean? It means that most of Michigan's firearm deer hunters might as well hang up their rifles if regulations are changed to protect the young bucks. Some say it will force hunters to harvest does and fawns. Will it? Is the DNR willing to issue all firearm hunters antlerless permits? I know better and so do all the unsuccessful applicants for "doe" permits. Just look at the vast "bucks only" areas in the 1991 permit application guide. I'm not faulting DNR biologists for conservative antlerless quotas. I'm just pointing out that Michigan has too many deer hunters to abandon a management system that now provides everyone a reasonable opportunity to bag a deer.

There are other problems that should be considered. When sighting a deer, how long does a firearm hunter have to make the decision to shoot or not to shoot? Unless you hunt over a bait pile, that time melts into seconds. Most good hunters identify the deer as a buck and then concentrate on making an accurate shot. To study the antlers seems out of the question to this old deer hunter. And if regulations require you to pass up the runty spikehorns and other small-antlered bucks, you are saving them to become the sires of your future deer herd! Yes,

Spring 1992   The Conservator   Page 5

genetics play a role in antler development.

Saving the little bucks is just the opposite of what you should be doing. A big buck that has lived through four or more deer seasons now does so by being smart enough to keep away from hunters.

Under the so-called "quality management," he would live longer just because you and other hunters let him go. This means that the quality deer get shot, the inferior deer live to reproduce. And while we're waiting for them to grow big antlers, they eat up a lot of scarce winter food — the food badly needed by does and fawns.

In my view, we had quality deer management in the 1930's, '40's, and '50's. We hunted together in small groups of three to five hunters and hunted most of the 16-day season. Michigan hunters, though fewer in number, got maximum recreation out of the deer herd. Shouldn't that be the deer management objective? Back in the early days, no one shot a buck the first hour and then packed up and went home. Hunters wouldn't think of leaving friends in the woods to fend for themselves. Even the Conservation Department approved by providing the opportunity for a group of hunters (four hunting from a camp) to buy an extra buck license to stay in woods legally and hunt with friends.

But deer hunting has changed since those good old days. Today, many hunters put too much emphasis on tagging a deer instead of the quality outdoor experience.

In my opinion, this emph is leads to baiting and other unethical behavio.. Sure, I know baiting is legal, but that doesn't make it right. Trophy hunting for big racks would just be another step in the wrong direction. Even some anti-hunters accept those who hunt for meat and I consider myself a meat hunter because I enjoy eating venison and other wild game. If I didn't, I wouldn't hunt. Most hunters will agree that the young bucks, does and fawns are the best eating, so, count on me to oppose regulations that will require hunters to pass up the 1-1/2-year-old bucks to enable them to grow up to be big bucks that sometimes are not fit to eat!

In over 50 years of deer hunting, I've had chances on only three big bucks. I know I could increase the odds by changing my hunting area, but I am highly successful right in my old stomping grounds, and I have no desire to change. And, as I said, little bucks are better to eat.

Of the two big-antlered deer I've bagged, one was shot for a doe to fill my "hunter choice" permit. Yes, I didn't see the 12-point antlers until he was down. The other, a deer I thought might be a six- or eight-pointer, turned out to be an 11-pointer weighing 196 pounds dressed.

It is apparent that I don't hunt over bait or out in open fields. My best set of antlers, the only one I've bothered to mount on a board of 40-plus bucks bagged, is a perfect eight-point rack with even tines — a beautiful set of antlers. What may surprise you is that this eight-point deer was only 1-1/2-years-old. Obviously, he carried superior genes and was a buck that everyone would be proud to bag.

Yes, under "quality management," hunters would shoot that one and let the runty spikes, three-, four-, and five-pointers go. In my opinion, "quality" buck management is a badly flawed idea. My advice to the DNR: concentrate on habitat management, the only long-term answer to maintaining good hunting — be it for deer, pheasants, grouse, or rabbits.

Page 10   The Conservator   **Spring 1992**

MCF's Past President proposes a swamp restoration project for whitetailed deer

by Ray Schofield

The *Michigan Conservation Foundation* has embarked on a deer-habitat initiative with the organization of two chapters of Michigan Whitetails. The Wexford-Missaukee Chapter and Grand Traverse Area Chapter promise exciting potential for raising local funds to improve habitat conditions for the white-tailed deer.

It is my opinion that efforts to improve habitat for deer should be directed at deer-wintering areas. Most of the lowland conifer swamps in the northern half of the Lower Peninsula are in poor condition due to over-browsing by deer and by the natural progression of tree growth.

Therefore, I recommend that we develop a proposed project aimed at restoring portions of the lowland-conifer swamps. Lou Verme, former Biologist-in-Charge of the Cusino Wildlife Experiment Station, came out with a swamp management plan in the early '60's. Robert Wood, who directed the deer range improvement program in the late '70's and early '80's, refined the work of Verme, Davenport, and others. However, little is being done to implement these ideas because of a lack of money.

With the new Michigan Whitetail Chapters, I believe we are well on the way to help solve the financial problems. We have already learned that these local deer hunters want to "get their teeth into worthwhile projects. The Wexford-Missaukee Group has already completed a tree-planting project and a burn project. With the support of the chapters in terms of financial resources and volunteer labor, we could have hugely successful swamp projects.

I propose that we develop a model swamp management project which could be applied throughout the northern two-thirds of Michigan. We don't want to compete with the Department of Natural Resources or the U.S. Forest Service, but we do want to supplement on-going work. Certainly, the knowledge and cooperation of working biologists and foresters will be needed in order to make any project successful.

It's obvious that deer will destroy new regeneration in areas cut, especially white cedar. With the vast areas now being fenced for Christmas tree plantations, it appears that we ought to be able to fence the deer OUT of areas treated. Deer will have to be excluded for about 20 years.

A swamp should be selected for work in each area where we have a chapter. Cooperation of the land managers and the local hunters will be essential. Several sites come readily to mind, but we must convince local land managers that the idea has merit. They must be willing to grant the necessary permissions and permits to allow these types of projects to go forward.

What will it cost? Let's look at a proposed 80-acre swamp cutting. That's an awfully big clearcut, but at the rate we're losing swamps and wetlands, perhaps feasible. In any case, for discussion purposes, an 80-acre parcel will produce results so let's use that size for now.

The area selected should be clear-cut with all the timber products sold to help defray costs. We hold back from sale the necessary posts to fence in the area. The area should be cut during the winter in order for the resident deer to get a big boost from the quality browsing produced. Volunteer labor from a good active local chapter could also be used to defray labor costs. We also have the potential for tapping Department of Social Services programs to obtain work assistance. Assuming no labor or posts cost, we could fence an 80-acre parcel for under $10,000.

There will be problems. First, the large clearcut will cause public relations problems. Next, we're bound to cut down some local deer hunter's favorite deer stand, but that could be resolved by building a couple of stiles.

The benefits would be well worth the cost. Not only would we be restoring the swamp timber type, but there will be almost immediate impact on snowshoe hare populations. Look for benefits for the ruffed grouse, too.

Let's leave some good swamp habitat for our grandchildren to enjoy.

About the Artist

THE AUTHOR WISHES TO ACKNOWLEDGE THE CONTRIBUTION OF the person who drew the sketch used for the cover. The artist is Edward (Ted) Herig from Canadian Lakes, near Mecosta, Michigan. Ted is a self-made naturalist who shares my love for the snowshoe hare and its primary habitat in this part of Michigan, the lowland conifer swamp. He is familiar with The Big Swamp.

Also, Ted is a recognized authority on Lepidoptera (butter-flies and moths). I appreciate him granting permission to use his picture on the cover of my book.

Order Information

To order additional copies of *The Big Swamp* forward the following information to:

5882 Long Bridge Road
Pentwater, Michigan 49449
e-mail: rscho@oceana.net

One copy of *The Big Swamp* costs $14.95 plus $3.50 for shipping and handling. If five or more books are ordered, please include $2.00 per book for shipping and handling.

Quantity discounts are available.

Number of books requested: _____

Total Enclosed: _____

Check and money order only, made payable to: Destiny

Please provide the following information:

Name: _____

Company Name: _____

Address: _____

_____

City/State/Zip: _____

Telephone: _____

Questions? Phone: (231) 869-8151

Thank you